DAY DREAMS

and other stories

Frank O'Connor was born in Cork in 1903. He had no formal education worth speaking of and his only real ambition was to become a writer. At the age of twelve he began to prepare a collected edition of his own works and, having learnt to speak Gaelic while very young, he studied his native poetry, music and legends. His literary career began with the translation of one of du Bellay's sonnets into Gaelic.

On release from imprisonment by the Free State Government for his part in the Civil War, O'Connor won a prize for his study of Turgenev, and subsequently had poetry, stories and translations published in the *Irish Statesman*. He caused great consternation in his native city by producing plays by Ibsen and Chekhov: a local clergyman remarked that the producer 'would go down in posterity at the head of the Pagan Dublin muses', and ladies in the local literary society threatened to resign when he mentioned the name of James Joyce.

O'Connor's other great interest was music, Mozart and the Irish composer Carolan being his favourites. By profession he was a librarian. He died in 1966 and will be long remembered as one of the great masters of short story writing.

DAY DREAMS
and other stories

FRANK O'CONNOR

Selected by Harriet Sheehy

PAN BOOKS LTD : LONDON

This collection selected from *The Stories of Frank O'Connor*, first published in Great Britain 1953 by Hamish Hamilton Ltd, and *Domestic Relations*, first published in Great Britain 1957 by Hamish Hamilton Ltd. This edition published 1973 by Pan Books Ltd, 33 Tothill Street, London SW1

ISBN 0 330 23556 7

*Printed and Bound in England by
Hazell Watson & Viney Ltd
Aylesbury, Bucks*

The following stories were printed – some of them in somewhat different form – in earlier collections of Frank O'Connor's stories: 'The Idealist', 'The Drunkard', 'The Masculine Principle' and 'Legal Aid' in *Traveller's Samples*; 'The Luceys' and 'The Long Road to Ummera' in *Crab Apple Jelly*; and 'Peasants' in *Bones of Contention*. 'The Man of the World', 'Day Dreams', 'The Pariah' and 'Expectation of Life' all appeared originally in the *New Yorker*.

CONTENTS

The Idealist

I don't know how it is about education, but it never seemed to do anything for me but get me into trouble.

Adventure stories weren't so bad, but as a kid I was very serious and preferred realism to romance. School stories were what I liked best, and, judged by our standards, these were romantic enough for anyone. The schools were English, so I suppose you couldn't expect anything else. They were always called 'the venerable pile', and there was usually a ghost in them; they were built in a square that was called 'the quad', and, according to the pictures, they were all clock-towers, spires, and pinnacles, like the lunatic asylum with us. The fellows in the stories were all good climbers, and got in and out of school at night on ropes made of knotted sheets. They dressed queerly; they wore long trousers, short, black jackets, and top hats. Whenever they did anything wrong they were given 'lines' in Latin. When it was a bad case, they were flogged and never showed any sign of pain; only the bad fellows, and they always said: 'Ow! Ow!'

Most of them were grand chaps who always stuck together and were great at football and cricket. They never told lies and wouldn't talk to anyone who did. If they were caught out and asked a point-blank question, they always told the truth, unless someone else was with them, and then even if they were to be expelled for it they wouldn't give his name, even if he was a thief, which, as a matter of fact, he frequently was. It was surprising in such good schools, with fathers who never gave less than five quid, the numbers of thieves there were. The fellows in our school hardly ever stole, though they only got a penny a week, and sometimes not even that, as when their fathers were on the booze and their mothers had to go to the pawn.

I worked hard at the football and cricket, though of course

we never had a proper football and the cricket we played was with a hurley stick against a wicket chalked on some wall. The officers in the barrack played proper cricket, and on summer evenings I used to go and watch them, like one of the souls in Purgatory watching the joys of Paradise.

Even so, I couldn't help being disgusted at the bad way things were run in our school. Our 'venerable pile' was a red-brick building without tower or pinnacle a fellow could climb, and no ghost at all: we had no team, so a fellow, no matter how hard he worked, could never play for the school, and, instead of giving you 'lines', Latin or any other sort, Murderer Moloney either lifted you by the ears or bashed you with a cane. When he got tired of bashing you on the hands he bashed you on the legs.

But these were only superficial things. What was really wrong was ourselves. The fellows sucked up to the masters and told them all that went on. If they were caught out in anything they tried to put the blame on someone else, even if it meant telling lies. When they were caned they snivelled and said it wasn't fair; drew back their hands as if they were terrified, so that the cane caught only the tips of their fingers, and then screamed and stood on one leg, shaking out their fingers in the hope of getting it counted as one. Finally they roared that their wrist was broken and crawled back to their desks with their hands squeezed under their armpits, howling. I mean you couldn't help feeling ashamed, imagining what chaps from a decent school would think if they saw it.

My own way to school led me past the barrack gate. In those peaceful days sentries never minded you going past the guard-room to have a look at the chaps drilling in the barrack square; if you came at dinnertime they even called you in and gave you plumduff and tea. Naturally, with such temptations I was often late. The only excuse, short of a letter from your mother, was to say you were at early Mass. The Murderer would never know whether you were or not, and if he did anything to you you could easily get him into trouble with the parish priest. Even as kids we knew who the real boss of the school was.

But after I started reading those confounded school stories I was never happy about saying I had been to Mass. It was a lie, and I knew that the chaps in the stories would have died sooner than tell it. They were all round me like invisible presences, and I hated to do anything which I felt they might disapprove of.

One morning I came in very late and rather frightened.

'What kept you till this hour, Delaney?' Murderer Moloney asked, looking at the clock.

I wanted to say I had been at Mass, but I couldn't. The invisible presences were all about me.

'I was delayed at the barrack, sir,' I replied in panic.

There was a faint titter from the class, and Moloney raised his brows in mild surprise. He was a big powerful man with fair hair and blue eyes and a manner that at times was deceptively mild.

'Oh, indeed,' he said, politely enough. 'And what delayed you?'

'I was watching the soldiers drilling, sir,' I said.

The class tittered again. This was a new line entirely for them.

'Oh,' Moloney said casually, 'I never knew you were such a military man. Hold out your hand!'

Compared with the laughter the slaps were nothing, and besides, I had the example of the invisible presences to sustain me. I did not flinch. I returned to my desk slowly and quietly without snivelling or squeezing my hands, and the Murderer looked after me, raising his brows again as though to indicate that this was a new line for him, too. But the others gaped and whispered as if I were some strange animal. At playtime they gathered about me, full of curiosity and excitement.

'Delaney, why did you say that about the barrack?'

'Because 'twas true,' I replied firmly. 'I wasn't going to tell him a lie.'

'What lie?'

'That I was at Mass.'

'Then couldn't you say you had to go on a message?'

'That would be a lie too.'

'Cripes, Delaney,' they said, 'you'd better mind yourself. The Murderer is in an awful wax. He'll massacre you.'

I knew that. I knew only too well that the Murderer's professional pride had been deeply wounded, and for the rest of the day I was on my best behaviour. But my best wasn't enough, for I underrated the Murderer's guile. Though he pretended to be reading, he was watching me the whole time.

'Delaney,' he said at last without raising his head from the book, 'was that you talking?'

' 'Twas, sir,' I replied in consternation.

The whole class laughed. They couldn't believe but that I was deliberately trailing my coat, and, of course, the laugh must have convinced him that I was. I suppose if people do tell you lies all day and every day, it soon becomes a sort of perquisite which you resent being deprived of.

'Oh,' he said, throwing down his book, 'we'll soon stop that.'

This time it was a tougher job, because he was really on his mettle. But so was I. I knew this was the testing-point for me, and if only I could keep my head I should provide a model for the whole class. When I had got through the ordeal without moving a muscle, and returned to my desk with my hands by my sides, the invisible presences gave me a great clap. But the visible ones were nearly as annoyed as the Murderer himself. After school half a dozen of them followed me down the school yard.

'Go on!' they shouted truculently. 'Shaping as usual!'

'I was not shaping.'

'You were shaping. You're always showing off. Trying to pretend he didn't hurt you – a blooming crybaby like you!'

'I wasn't trying to pretend,' I shouted, even then resisting the temptation to nurse my bruised hands. 'Only decent fellows don't cry over every little pain like kids.'

'Go on!' they bawled after me. 'You ould idiot!' And, as I went down the school lane, still trying to keep what the stories called 'a stiff upper lip', and consoling myself with the thought that my torment was over until next morning, I heard their mocking voices after me.

'Loony Larry! Yah, Loony Larry!'

I realized that if I was to keep on terms with the invisible presences I should have to watch my step at school.

So I did, all through that year. But one day an awful thing happened. I was coming in from the yard, and in the porch outside our schoolroom I saw a fellow called Gorman taking something from a coat on the rack. I always described Gorman to myself as 'the black sheep of the school'. He was a fellow I disliked and feared; a handsome, sulky, spoiled, and sneering lout. I paid no attention to him because I had escaped for a few moments into my dream-world in which fathers never gave less than fivers and the honour of the school was always saved by some quiet, unassuming fellow like myself – 'a dark horse', as the stories called him.

'Who are you looking at?' Gorman asked threateningly.

'I wasn't looking at anyone,' I replied with an indignant start.

'I was only getting a pencil out of my coat,' he added, clenching his fists.

'Nobody said you weren't,' I replied, thinking that this was a very queer subject to start a row about.

'You'd better not, either,' he snarled. 'You can mind your own business.'

'You mind yours!' I retorted, purely for the purpose of saving face. 'I never spoke to you at all.'

And that, so far as I was concerned, was the end of it.

But after playtime the Murderer, looking exceptionally serious, stood before the class, balancing a pencil in both hands.

'Everyone who left the classroom this morning, stand out!' he called. Then he lowered his head and looked at us from under his brows. 'Mind now, I said everyone!'

I stood out with the others, including Gorman. We were all very puzzled.

'Did you take anything from a coat on the rack this morning?' the Murderer asked, laying a heavy, hairy paw on Gorman's shoulder and staring menacingly into his eyes.

'Me, sir?' Gorman exclaimed innocently. 'No, sir.'

'Did you see anyone else doing it?'

'No, sir.'

'You?' he asked another lad, but even before he reached me at all I realized why Gorman had told the lie and wondered frantically what I should do.

'You?' he asked me, and his big red face was close to mine, his blue eyes were only a few inches away, and the smell of his toilet soap was in my nostrils. My panic made me say the wrong thing as though I had planned it.

'I didn't take anything, sir,' I said in a low vonce.

'Did you see someone else do it?' he asked, raising his brows and showing quite plainly that he had noticed my evasion. 'Have you a tongue in your head?' he shouted suddenly, and the whole class, electrified, stared at me. 'You?' he added curtly to the next boy as though he had lost interest in me.

'No, sir.'

'Back to your desks, the rest of you!' he ordered. 'Delaney, you stay here.'

He waited till everyone was seated again before going on.

'Turn out your pockets.'

I did, and a half-stifled giggle rose, which the Murderer quelled with a thunderous glance. Even for a small boy I had pockets that were museums in themselves: the purpose of half the things I brought to light I couldn't have explained myself. They were antiques, prehistoric and unlabelled. Among them was a school story borrowed the previous evening from a queer fellow who chewed paper as if it were gum. The Murderer reached out for it, and holding it at arm's length, shook it out with an expression of deepening disgust as he noticed the nibbled corners and margins.

'Oh,' he said disdainfully, 'so this is how you waste your time! What do you do with this rubbish – eat it?'

''Tisn't mine, sir,' I said against the laugh that sprang up. 'I borrowed it.'

'Is that what you did with the money?' he asked quickly, his fat head on one side.

'Money?' I repeated in confusion. 'What money?'

'The shilling that was stolen from Flanagan's overcoat this morning.'

(Flanagan was a little hunchback whose people coddled him;

no one else in the school would have possessed that much money.)

'I never took Flanagan's shilling,' I said, beginning to cry, 'and you have no right to say I did.'

'I have the right to say you're the most impudent and defiant puppy in the school,' he replied, his voice hoarse with rage, 'and I wouldn't put it past you. What else can anyone expect and you reading this dirty, rotten, filthy rubbish?' And he tore my school story in halves and flung them to the farthest corner of the classroom. 'Dirty, filthy, English rubbish! Now, hold out your hand.'

This time the invisible presences deserted me. Hearing themselves described in these contemptuous terms, they fled. The Murderer went mad in the way people do whenever they're up against something they don't understand. Even the other fellows were shocked, and, heaven knows, they had little sympathy with me.

'You should put the police on him,' they advised me later in the playground. 'He lifted the cane over his shoulder. He could get the jail for that.'

'But why didn't you say you didn't see anyone?' asked the eldest, a fellow called Spillane.

'Because I did,' I said, beginning to sob all over again at the memory of my wrongs. 'I saw Gorman.'

'Gorman?' Spillane echoed incredulously. 'Was it Gorman took Flanagan's money? And why didn't you say so?'

'Because it wouldn't be right,' I sobbed.

'Why wouldn't it be right?'

'Because Gorman should have told the truth himself,' I said. 'And if this was a proper school he'd be sent to Coventry.'

'He'd be sent where?'

'Coventry. No one would ever speak to him again.'

'But why would Gorman tell the truth if he took the money?' Spillane asked as you'd speak to a baby. 'Jay, Delaney,' he added pityingly, 'you're getting madder and madder. Now, look at what you're after bringing on yourself!'

Suddenly Gorman came lumbering up, red and angry.

'Delaney,' he shouted threateningly, 'did you say I took Flanagan's money?'

Gorman, though I of course didn't realize it, was as much at sea as Moloney and the rest. Seeing me take all that punishment rather than give him away, he concluded that I must be more afraid of him than of Moloney, and that the proper thing to do was to make me more so. He couldn't have come at a time when I cared less for him. I didn't even bother to reply but lashed out with all my strength at his brutal face. This was the last thing he expected. He screamed, and his hand came away from his face, all blood. Then he threw off his satchel and came at me, but at the same moment a door opened behind us and a lame teacher called Murphy emerged. We all ran like mad and the fight was forgotten.

It didn't remain forgotten, though. Next morning after prayers the Murderer scowled at me.

'Delaney, were you fighting in the yard after school yesterday?'

For a second or two I didn't reply. I couldn't help feeling that it wasn't worth it. But before the invisible presences fled for ever, I made another effort.

'I was, sir,' I said, and this time there wasn't even a titter. I was out of my mind. The whole class knew it and was awe-stricken.

'Who were you fighting?'

'I'd sooner not say, sir,' I replied, hysteria beginning to well up in me. It was all very well for the invisible presences, but they hadn't to deal with the Murderer.

'Who was he fighting with?' he asked lightly, resting his hands on the desk and studying the ceiling.

'Gorman, sir,' replied three or four voices – as easy as that!

'Did Gorman hit him first?'

'No, sir. He hit Gorman first.'

'Stand out,' he said, taking up the cane. 'Now,' he added, going up to Gorman, 'you take this and hit him. And make sure you hit him hard,' he went on, giving Gorman's arm an encouraging squeeze. 'He thinks he's a great fellow. You show him now what we think of him.'

Gorman came towards me with a broad grin. He thought it a great joke. The class thought it a great joke. They began to roar with laughter. Even the Murderer permitted himself a modest grin at his own cleverness.

'Hold out your hand,' he said to me.

I didn't. I began to feel trapped and a little crazy.

'Hold out your hand, I say,' he shouted, beginning to lose his temper.

'I will not,' I shouted back, losing all control of myself.

'You what?' he cried incredulously, dashing at me round the classroom with his hand raised as though to strike me. 'What's that you said, you dirty little thief?'

'I'm not a thief, I'm not a thief,' I screamed. 'And if he comes near me I'll kick the shins off him. You have no right to give him that cane, and you have no right to call me a thief either. If you do it again, I'll go down to the police and then we'll see who the thief is.'

'You refused to answer my questions,' he roared, and if I had been in my right mind I should have known he had suddenly taken fright; probably the word 'police' had frightened him.

'No,' I said through my sobs, 'and I won't answer them now either. I'm not a spy.'

'Oh,' he retorted with a sarcastic sniff, 'so that's what you call a spy, Mr Delaney?'

'Yes, and that's what they all are, all the fellows here – dirty spies! – but I'm not going to spy for you. You can do your own spying.'

'That's enough now, that's enough!' he said, raising his fat hand almost beseechingly. 'There's no need to lose control of yourself, my dear young fellow, and there's no need whatever to screech like that. 'Tis most unmanly. Go back to your seat now and I'll talk to you another time.'

I obeyed, but I did no work. No one else did much either. The hysteria had spread to the class. I alternated between fits of exultation at my own successful defiance of the Murderer, and panic at the prospect of his revenge; and at each change of mood I put my face in my hands and sobbed again. The Murderer didn't even order me to stop. He didn't so much as look at me.

After that I was the hero of the school for the whole afternoon. Gorman tried to resume the fight, but Spillane ordered him away contemptuously – a fellow who had taken the master's cane to another had no status. But that wasn't the sort of hero I wanted to be. I preferred something less sensational.

Next morning I was in such a state of panic that I didn't know how I should face school at all. I dawdled, between two minds as to whether or not I should mitch. The silence of the school lane and yard awed me. I had made myself late as well.

'What kept you, Delaney?' the Murderer asked quietly.

I knew it was no good.

'I was at Mass, sir.'

'All right. Take your seat.'

He seemed a bit surprised. What I had not realized was the incidental advantage of our system over the English one. By this time half a dozen of his pets had brought the Murderer the true story of Flanagan's shilling, and if he didn't feel a monster he probably felt a fool.

But by that time I didn't care. In my school sack I had another story. Not a school story this time, though. School stories were a washout. 'Bang! Bang!' – that was the only way to deal with men like the Murderer. 'The only good teacher is a dead teacher.'

The Drunkard

It was a terrible blow to Father when Mr Dooley on the terrace died. Mr Dooley was a commercial traveller with two sons in the Dominicans and a car of his own, so socially he was miles ahead of us, but he had no false pride. Mr Dooley was an intellectual, and, like all intellectuals, the thing he loved best was conversation, and in his own limited way Father was a well-read man and could appreciate an intelligent talker. Mr Dooley was remarkably intelligent. Between business acquaintances and clerical contacts, there was very little he didn't know about what went on in town, and evening after evening he crossed the road to our gate to explain to Father the news behind the news. He had a low, palavering voice and a knowing smile, and Father would listen in astonishment, giving him a conversational lead now and again, and then stump triumphantly in to Mother with his face aglow and ask: 'Do you know what Mr Dooley is after telling me?' Ever since, when somebody has given me some bit of information off the record I have found myself on the point of asking: 'Was it Mr Dooley told you that?'

Till I actually saw him laid out in his brown shroud with the rosary beads entwined between his waxy fingers I did not take the report of his death seriously. Even then I felt there must be a catch and that some summer evening Mr Dooley must reappear at our gate to give us the lowdown on the next world. But Father was very upset, partly because Mr Dooley was about one age with himself, a thing that always gives a distinctly personal turn to another man's demise; partly because now he would have no one to tell him what dirty work was behind the latest scene at the Corporation. You could count on your fingers the number of men in Blarney Lane who read the papers as Mr Dooley did, and none of these would have over-

looked the fact that Father was only a labouring man. Even
Sullivan, the carpenter, a mere nobody, thought he was a cut
above Father. It was certainly a solemn event.

'Half past two to the Curragh,' Father said meditatively,
putting down the paper.

'But you're not thinking of going to the funeral?' Mother
asked in alarm.

' 'Twould be expected,' Father said, scenting opposition. 'I
wouldn't give it to say to them.'

'I think,' said Mother with suppressed emotion, 'it will be as
much as anyone will expect if you go to the chapel with him.'

('Going to the chapel', of course, was one thing, because the
body was removed after work, but going to a funeral meant the
loss of a half-day's pay.)

'The people hardly know us,' she added.

'God between us and all harm,' Father replied with dignity,
'we'd be glad if it was our own turn.'

To give Father his due, he was always ready to lose a half-
day for the sake of an old neighbour. It wasn't so much that he
liked funerals as that he was a conscientious man who did as he
would be done by; and nothing could have consoled him so
much for the prospect of his own death as the assurance of a
worthy funeral. And, to give Mother her due, it wasn't the half-
day's pay she begrudged, badly as we could afford it.

Drink, you see, was Father's great weakness. He could keep
steady for months, even for years, at a stretch, and while he did
he was as good as gold. He was first up in the morning and
brought the mother a cup of tea in bed, stayed at home in the
evenings and read the paper; saved money and bought himself
a new blue serge suit and bowler hat. He laughed at the folly
of men who, week in week out, left their hard-earned money
with the publicans; and sometimes, to pass an idle hour, he
took pencil and paper and calculated precisely how much he
saved each week through being a teetotaller. Being a natural
optimist he sometimes continued this calculation through the
whole span of his prospective existence and the total was
breathtaking. He would die worth hundreds.

If I had only known it, this was a bad sign; a sign he was

becoming stuffed up with spiritual pride and imagining himself better than his neighbours. Sooner or later, the spiritual
pride grew till it called for some form of celebration. Then he
took a drink – not whiskey, of course; nothing like that – just
a glass of some harmless drink like lager beer. That was the
end of Father. By the time he had taken the first he already
realized that he had made a fool of himself, took a second to
forget it and a third to forget that he couldn't forget, and at
last came home reeling drunk. From this on it was 'The Drunkard's Progress', as in the moral prints. Next day he stayed in
from work with a sick head while Mother went off to make his
excuses at the works, and inside a fortnight he was poor and
savage and despondent again. Once he began he drank steadily
through everything down to the kitchen clock. Mother and I
knew all the phases and dreaded all the dangers. Funerals were
one.

'I have to go to Dunphy's to do a half-day's work,' said
Mother in distress. 'Who's to look after Larry?'

'I'll look after Larry,' Father said graciously. 'The little walk
will do him good.'

There was no more to be said, though we all knew I didn't
need anyone to look after me, and that I could quite well have
stayed at home and looked after Sonny, but I was being at-
tached to the party to act as a brake on Father. As a brake I
had never achieved anything, but Mother still had great faith
in me.

Next day, when I got home from school, Father was there
before me and made a cup of tea for both of us. He was very
good at tea, but too heavy in the hand for anything else; the
way he cut bread was shocking. Afterwards we went down the
hill to the church, Father wearing his best blue serge and a
bowler cocked to one side of his head with the least suggestion
of the masher. To his great joy he discovered Peter Crowley
among the mourners. Peter was another danger signal, as I
knew well from certain experiences after Mass on Sunday
morning: a mean man, as Mother said, who only went to
funerals for the free drinks he could get at them. It turned out
that he hadn't even known Mr Dooley! But Father had a sort

of contemptuous regard for him as one of the foolish people who wasted their good money in public-houses when they could be saving it. Very little of his own money Peter Crowley wasted!

It was an excellent funeral from Father's point of view. He had it all well studied before we set off after the hearse in the afternoon sunlight.

'Five carriages!' he exclaimed. 'Five carriages and sixteen covered cars! There's one alderman, two councillors and 'tis unknown how many priests. I didn't see a funeral like this from the road since Willie Mack, the publican died.'

'Ah, he was well liked,' said Crowley in his husky voice.

'My goodness, don't I know that?' snapped Father. 'Wasn't the man my best friend? Two nights before he died – only two nights – he was over telling me the goings-on about the housing contract. Them fellows in the Corporation are night and day robbers. But even I never imagined he was as well connected as that.'

Father was stepping out like a boy, pleased with everything: the other mourners, and the fine houses along Sunday's Well. I knew the danger signals were there in full force: a sunny day, a fine funeral, and a distinguished company of clerics and public men were bringing out all the natural vanity and flightiness of Father's character. It was with something like genuine pleasure that he saw his old friend lowered into the grave; with the sense of having performed a duty and the pleasant awareness that however much he would miss poor Mr Dooley in the long summer evenings, it was he and not poor Mr Dooley who would do the missing.

'We'll be making tracks before they break up,' he whispered to Crowley as the gravediggers tossed in the first shovelfuls of clay, and away he went, hopping like a goat from grassy hump to hump. The drivers, who were probably in the same state as himself, though without months of abstinence to put an edge on it, looked up hopefully.

'Are they nearly finished, Mick?' bawled one.

'All over now bar the last prayers,' trumpeted Father in the tone of one who brings news of great rejoicing.

The carriages passed us in a lather of dust several hundred yards from the public-house, and Father, whose feet gave him trouble in hot weather, quickened his pace, looking nervously over his shoulder for any sign of the main body of mourners crossing the hill. In a crowd like that a man might be kept waiting.

When we did reach the pub the carriages were drawn up outside, and solemn men in black ties were cautiously bringing out consolation to mysterious females whose hands reached out modestly from behind the drawn blinds of the coaches. Inside the pub there were only the drivers and a couple of shawly women. I felt if I was to act as a brake at all, this was the time, so I pulled Father by the coat-tails.

'Dadda, can't we go home now?' I asked.

'Two minutes now,' he said, beaming affectionately. 'Just a bottle of lemonade and we'll go home.'

This was a bribe, and I knew it, but I was always a child of weak character. Father ordered lemonade and two pints. I was thirsty and swallowed my drink at once. But that wasn't Father's way. He had long months of abstinence behind him and an eternity of pleasure before. He took out his pipe, blew through it, filled it, and then lit it with loud pops, his eyes bulging above it. After that he deliberately turned his back on the pint, leaned one elbow on the counter in the attitude of a man who did not know there was a pint behind him, and deliberately brushed the tobacco from his palms. He had settled down for the evening. He was steadily working through all the important funerals he had ever attended. The carriages departed and the minor mourners drifted in till the pub was half full.

'Dadda,' I said, pulling his coat again, 'can't we go home now?'

'Ah, your mother won't be in for a long time yet,' he said benevolently enough. 'Run out in the road and play, can't you?'

It struck me as very cool, the way grown-ups assumed that you could play all by yourself on a strange road. I began to get bored as I had so often been bored before. I knew Father was quite capable of lingering there till nightfall. I knew I might have to bring him home, blind drunk, down Blarney Lane, with all the old women at their doors, saying: 'Mick Delaney is on it again.' I knew that my mother would be half crazy with anxiety; that next day Father wouldn't go out to work; and before the end of the week she would be running down to the pawn with the clock under her shawl. I could never get over the lonesomeness of the kitchen without a clock.

I was still thirsty. I found if I stood on tiptoe I could just reach Father's glass, and the idea occurred to me that it would be interesting to know what the contents were like. He had his back to it and wouldn't notice. I took down the glass and sipped cautiously. It was a terrible disappointment. I was astonished that he could even drink such stuff. It looked as if he had never tried lemonade.

I should have advised him about lemonade but he was holding forth himself in great style. I heard him say that bands were a great addition to a funeral. He put his arms in the position of someone holding a rifle in reverse and hummed a few bars of Chopin's Funeral March. Crowley nodded reverently. I took a longer drink and began to see that porter might have its advantages. I felt pleasantly elevated and philosophic. Father hummed a few bars of the Dead March in *Saul*. It was a nice pub and a very fine funeral, and I felt sure that poor Mr Dooley in Heaven must be highly gratified. At the same time I thought they might have given him a band. As Father said, bands were a great addition.

But the wonderful thing about about porter was the way it made you stand aside, or rather float aloft like a cherub rolling on a cloud, and watch yourself with your legs crossed, leaning against a bar counter, not worrying about trifles but thinking deep, serious, grown-up thoughts about life and death. Looking at yourself like that, you couldn't help thinking after a while how funny you looked, and suddenly you got embarrassed and wanted to giggle. But by the time I had finished the pint, that phase too had passed; I found it hard to put back the glass, the counter seemed to have grown so high. Melancholia was supervening again.

'Well,' Father said reverently, reaching behind him for his

drink, 'God rest the poor man's soul, wherever he is!' He stopped, looked first at the glass, and then at the people round him. 'Hello,' he said in a fairly good-humoured tone, as if he were just prepared to consider it a joke, even if it was in bad taste, 'who was at this?'

There was silence for a moment while the publican and the old women looked first at Father and then at his glass.

'There was no one at it, my good man,' one of the women said with an offended air. 'Is it robbers you think we are?'

'Ah, there's no one here would do a thing like that, Mick,' said the publican in a shocked tone.

'Well, someone did it,' said Father, his smile beginning to wear off.

'If they did, they were them that were nearer it,' said the woman darkly, giving me a dirty look; and at the same moment the truth began to dawn on Father. I suppose I must have looked a bit starry-eyed. He bent and shook me.

'Are you all right, Larry?' he asked in alarm.

Peter Cowley looked down at me and grinned.

'Could you beat that?' he exclaimed in a husky voice.

I could, and without difficulty. I started to get sick. Father jumped back in holy terror that I might spoil his good suit, and hastily opened the back door.

'Run! run! run!' he shouted.

I saw the sunlit wall outside with the ivy overhanging it, and ran. The intention was good but the performance was exaggerated, because I lurched right into the wall, hurting it badly, as it seemed to me. Being always very polite, I said 'Pardon' before the second bout came on me. Father, still concerned for his suit, came up behind and cautiously held me while I got sick.

'That's a good boy!' he said encouragingly. 'You'll be grand when you get that up.'

Begor, I was not grand! Grand was the last thing I was. I gave one unmerciful wail out of me as he steered me back to the pub and put me sitting on the bench near the shawlies. They drew themselves up with an offended air, still sore at the suggestion that they had drunk his pint.

'God help us!' moaned one, looking pityingly at me, 'isn't it the likes of them would be fathers?'

'Mick,' said the publican in alarm, spraying sawdust on my tracks, 'that child isn't supposed to be in here at all. You'd better take him home quick in case a bobby would see him.'

'Merciful God!' whimpered Father, raising his eyes to heaven and clapping his hands silently as he only did when distraught, 'what misfortune was on me? Or what will his mother say? ... If women might stop at home and look after their children themselves!' he added in a snarl for the benefit of the shawlies. 'Are them carriages all gone, Bill?'

'The carriages are finished long ago, Mick,' replied the publican.

'I'll take him home,' Father said despairingly ... 'I'll never bring you out again,' he threatened me. 'Here,' he added, giving me the clean handkerchief from his breast pocket, 'put that over your eye.'

The blood on the handkerchief was the first indication I got that I was cut, and instantly my temple began to throb and I set up another howl.

'Whisht, whisht, whisht!' Father said testily, steering me out the door. 'One'd think you were killed. That's nothing. We'll wash it when we get home.'

'Steady now, old scout!' Cowley said, taking the other side of me. 'You'll be all right in a minute.'

I never met two men who knew less about the effects of drink. The first breath of fresh air and the warmth of the sun made me groggier than ever and I pitched and rolled between wind and tide till Father started to whimper again.

'God Almighty, and the whole road out! What misfortune was on me didn't stop at my work! Can't you walk straight?'

I couldn't. I saw plain enough that, coaxed by the sunlight, every woman old and young in Blarney Lane was leaning over her half-door or sitting on her doorstep. They all stopped gabbling to gape at the strange spectacle of two sober, middle-aged men bringing home a drunken small boy with a cut over his eye. Father, torn between the shamefast desire to get me

home as quick as he could, and the neighbourly need to explain
that it wasn't his fault, finally halted outside Mrs Roche's.
There was a gang of old women outside a door at the opposite
side of the road. I didn't like the look of them from the first.
They seemed altogether too interested in me. I leaned against
the wall of Mrs Roche's cottage with my hands in my trouser
pockets, thinking mournfully of poor Mr Dooley in his cold
grave on the Curragh, who would never walk down the road
again, and, with great feeling, I began to sing a favourite song
of Father's.

> *Though lost to Mononia and cold in the grave*
> *He returns to Kincora no more.*

'Wisha, the poor child!' Mrs Roche said. 'Haven't he a
lovely voice, God bless him!'

That was what I thought myself, so I was the more surprised
when Father said 'Whisht!' and raised a threatening finger at
me. He didn't seem to realize the appropriateness of the song,
so I sang louder than ever.

'Whisht, I tell you!' he snapped, and then tried to work up a
smile for Mrs Roche's benefit. 'We're nearly home now. I'll
carry you the rest of the way.'

But, drunk and all as I was, I knew better than to be carried home ignominiously like that.

'Now,' I said severely, 'can't you leave me alone? I can
walk all right. 'Tis only my head. All I want is a rest.'

'But you can rest at home in bed,' he said viciously, trying to
pick me up, and I knew by the flush on his face that he was
very vexed.

'Ah, Jasus,' I said crossly, 'what do I want to go home for?
Why the hell can't you leave me alone?'

For some reason the gang of old women at the other side of
the road thought this very funny. They nearly split their sides
over it. A gassy fury began to expand in me at the thought that
a fellow couldn't have a drop taken without the whole neighbourhood coming out to make game of him.

'Who are ye laughing at?' I shouted, clenching my fists at

them. 'I'll make ye laugh at the other side of yeer faces if ye don't let me pass.'

They seemed to think this funnier still; I had never seen such ill-mannered people.

'Go away, ye bloody bitches!' I said.

'Whisht, whisht, whisht, I tell you!' snarled Father, abandoning all pretence of amusement and dragging me along behind him by the hand. I was maddened by the women's shrieks of laughter. I was maddened by Father's bullying. I tried to dig in my heels but he was too powerful for me, and I could only see the women by looking back over my shoulder.

'Take care or I'll come back and show ye!' I shouted. 'I'll teach ye to let decent people pass. Fitter for ye to stop at home and wash yeer dirty faces.'

' 'Twill be all over the road,' whimpered Father. 'Never again, never again, not if I lived to be a thousand!'

To this day I don't know whether he was forswearing me or the drink. By way of a song suitable to my heroic mood I bawled 'The Boys of Wexford', as he dragged me in home. Crowley, knowing he was not safe, made off and Father undressed me and put me to bed. I couldn't sleep because of the whirling in my head. It was very unpleasant, and I got sick again. Father came in with a wet cloth and mopped up after me. I lay in a fever, listening to him chopping sticks to start a fire. After that I heard him lay the table.

Suddenly the front door banged open and Mother stormed in with Sonny in her arms, not her usual gentle, timid self, but a wild, raging woman. It was clear that she had heard it all from the neighbours.

'Mick Delaney,' she cried hysterically, 'what did you do to my son?'

'Whisht, woman, whisht, whisht!' he hissed, dancing from one foot to the other. 'Do you want the whole road to hear?'

'Ah,' she said with a horrifying laugh, 'the road knows all about it by this time. The road knows the way you filled your unfortunate innocent child with drink to make sport for you and that other rotten, filthy brute.'

'But I gave him no drink,' he shouted, aghast at the horrify-

ing interpretation the neighbours had chosen to give his misfortune. 'He took it while my back was turned. What the hell
do you think I am?'

'Ah,' she replied bitterly, 'everyone knows what you are now.
God forgive you, wasting our hard-earned few ha'pence on
drink, and bringing up your child to be a drunken corner-boy
like yourself.'

Then she swept into the bedroom and threw herself on her
knees by the bed. She moaned when she saw the gash over my
eye. In the kitchen Sonny set up a loud bawl on his own, and a
moment later Father appeared in the bedroom door with his
cap over his eyes, wearing an expression of the most intense
self-pity.

'That's a nice way to talk to me after all I went through,' he
whined. 'That's a nice accusation, that I was drinking. Not one
drop of drink crossed my lips the whole day. How could it
when he drank it all? I'm the one that ought to be pitied, with
my day ruined on me, and I after being made a show for the
whole road.'

But next morning, when he got up and went out quietly
to work with his dinner-basket, Mother threw herself on me in
the bed and kissed me. It seemed it was all my doing, and I
was being given a holiday till my eye got better.

'My brave little man!' she said with her eyes shining. 'It was
God did it you were there. You were his guardian angel.'

The Masculine Principle

Myles Reilly was a building contractor in a small way of business that would never be any larger owing to the difficulty he found in doing sums. For a man of expansive nature sums are hell; they narrow and degrade the mind. And Myles was expansive, a heavy, shambling man, always verging on tears or laughter, with a face like a sunset, and something almost physically boneless about his make-up. A harassed man too, for all his fat, because he was full of contradictory impulses. He was a first-rate worker, but there was no job, however fascinating, which he wouldn't leave for the sake of a chat, and no conversation, however delightful, which did not conceal a secret sense of guilt. 'God, I promised Gaffney I'd be out of that place by Saturday, Joe. I know I ought to be going; I declare to my God I ought, but I love an intelligent talk. That's the thing I miss most, Joe – someone intelligent to talk to.'

But even if he was no good at sums he was great at daughters. He had three of these, all stunners, but he never recognized his real talent and continued to lament the son he wanted. This was very shortsighted of him because there wasn't a schoolboy in town who wouldn't raise his cap to Myles in hopes of impressing his spotty visage on him, so that one day he might say to his daughters, 'Who's that charming fellow from St Joseph's Terrace – best-mannered boy in the town. Why don't we ever have him round here?' There was no recorded instance of his saying anything of the sort, which might have been as well, because if the boys' mothers didn't actually imply that the girls were fast, they made no bones about saying they were flighty. Mothers, unfortunately, are like that.

They were three grand girls. Brigid, the eldest, was tall and bossy like a reverend mother; Joan, the youngest, was small and ingratiating, but Evelyn was a bit of a problem. She seemed to have given up early any hope of competing with her sisters and resigned herself to being the next best thing to the missing son. She slouched, she swore, she drank, she talked with the local accent which her sisters had discarded; and her matey air inspired fierce passions in cripples, out-of-works, and middle-aged widowers, who wrote her formal proposals beginning: 'Dearest Miss Reilly, since the death of my dear wife RIP five years ago I gave up all hopes of meeting another lady that would mean the same to me till I had the good fortune to meet your charming self. I have seven children; the eldest is eighteen and will soon be leaving home and the other six are no trouble.'

Then Jim Piper came on the scene. Nobody actually remembered inviting him, nobody pressed him to come again, but he came and hung on. It was said that he wasn't very happy at home. He was a motor mechanic by trade. His mother kept a huxter shop, and in her spare time was something of a collector, mostly of shillings and sixpenny bits. This was supposed to be why Jim was so glad to get out of the house. But, as Father Ring was the first to discover, Jim had a tough streak too.

Father Ring was also a collector. Whatever pretty girls he had banished from his conscious mind came back to him in dreams disguised as pound notes, except the plainer, coarser types who took the form of ten-shilling notes. Mrs Piper was shocked by this, and when Father Ring came for his dues, she fought him with all the guile and passion of a fellow collector. When Jim was out of his time Father Ring decided that it would be much more satisfactory to deal with him; a nice easy-going boy with nothing of the envy and spite of his mother.

Jim agreed at once to pay the dues himself. He took out his wallet and produced a ten-shilling note. Now, ten shillings was a lot of money to a working man, and at least four times what his mother had ever paid, but the sight of it sent a fastidious shudder through Father Ring. As I say, he associated it with the coarser type of female.

'Jim,' he said roguishly, 'I think you could make that a pound.'

'I'm afraid I couldn't, Father,' Jim replied respectfully, trying to look Father Ring in the eye, a thing that was never easy.

'Of course, Jim,' Father Ring said in a tone of grief, ' 'tis all one to me what you pay; I won't touch a penny of it; but at the same time, I'd only be getting into trouble taking it from you. 'Twouldn't be wishing to me.'

'I dare say not, Father,' said Jim. Though he grew red he behaved with perfect respect. 'I won't press you.'

So Father Ring went off in the lofty mood of a man who has defended a principle at a great sacrifice to himself, but that very night he began to brood and he continued to brood till that sickly looking voluptuary of a ten-shilling note took on all the radiance and charm of a virgin of seventeen. Back he went to Jim for it.

'Don't say a word to anybody,' he whispered confidentially. 'I'll put that through.'

'At Christmas you will, Father,' Jim said with a faint smile, apparently quite unaware of the favour Father Ring thought he was doing him. 'The Easter dues were offered and refused.'

Father Ring flushed and almost struck him. He was a passionate man; the lovers' quarrel over, the reconciliation complete, the consummation at hand, he saw her go off to spend the night with another man – his beautiful, beautiful ten-shilling note!

'I beg your pardon,' he snapped. 'I thought I was talking to a Christian.'

It was more than a man should be asked to bear. He had been too hasty, too hasty! A delicate, high-spirited creature like her! Father Ring went off to brood again, and the more he brooded, the dafter his schemes became. He thought of having a special collection for the presbytery roof but he felt the bishop would probably only send down the diocesan architect. Bishops, like everything else, were not what they used to be; there was no gravity in them, and excommunication was practically unknown. A fortnight later he was back to Jim.

'Jim, boy,' he whispered, 'I'll be wanting you for a concert at the end of the month.'

Now, Jim wasn't really much of a singer; only a man in the throes of passion would have considered him a singer at all, but

such was his contrariness that he became convinced that Father
Ring was only out to get his money, by hook or crook.

'All right, Father,' he said smoothly. 'What's the fee?'

'Fee?' gasped Father Ring. 'What fee?'

'The fee for singing, Father.'

And not one note would Jim sing without being paid for it!
It was the nearest thing to actual free-thinking Father Ring
had ever encountered, the reflection among the laity of the
bishops' cowardice, and he felt that at last he understood the
sort of man Voltaire must have been. A fee!

Myles Reilly loved telling that story, not because he was
against the Church but because he was expansive by temperament and felt himself jailed by the mean-spiritedness of life
about him. 'God, I love a man!' he muttered and turned to his
pint. 'A man, not a pincushion,' he added, drinking and looking
fiercely away. He liked Jim because he was what he would have
wished a son of his own to be. When Evelyn and Jim became
engaged he was deeply moved. 'You picked the best of the
bunch,' he muttered to Jim with tears in his eyes. 'God, I'm
not criticizing any of them because I love them all, but Evvie
is out on her own. She may have a bit of a temper, but what
good is anyone without it?'

He said the same things about Jim to the girls, but they,
being romantic, didn't pay much heed to him, even Evelyn
herself. He had no patience with the sort of fellows they
knocked round with; counter-jumpers and bank clerks with
flannel bags and sports coats; tennis-players, tea-party gents
carrying round plates of sandwiches – 'Will you have some of
this or some of that, please?' God Almighty, how could anyone put up with it? When Jim started bringing Evelyn ten shillings a week out of his wages to put in her Post Office account
towards the wedding, Myles drew the lesson for them. There
was the good, steady tradesman – the man, the *man* – not like
the sports coats and the flannel bags who'd have been more
likely to touch them for the ten bob. When Evelyn had two
hundred saved he'd build a house for them himself. It would be
like no house they ever saw; modern, if you wished, and with
every labour-saving device, but it would be a house, a *house*,

not a bloody concrete box. The girls listened to him with amusement; they always enjoyed their father's temperamental grumblings and moanings without ever taking them seriously.

'You don't know what you're letting yourself in for,' Evelyn said dryly to Jim. 'You may be engaged to me but you're going to marry my da. Greatest mistake anyone could make, getting too thick with their in-laws.'

In fact, Jim was more popular with father than with daughters. They, of course, were not haunted by the image of a son they could not have. Evelyn liked Jim well enough, and, given a chance, she might even have loved him, but the sense of inferiority towards her sisters left her peculiarly vulnerable to their criticisms. They didn't understand what she could see in Jim, a poor fish of a fellow who only came to their house because he wasn't happy at home. The ten shillings a week put the finishing touches to him. How any girl of feeling could go with a man who saved ten shillings a week towards his wedding was beyond them. Evelyn defended him as best she could, but secretly she felt they were right, and that as usual she had got the second best out of life, a decent poor slob of a mechanic whom her sisters would turn up their noses at.

Then, at Christmas, she went out to do the shopping with the week's housekeeping in her purse, ran into a crowd of fellows home from Dublin for the holidays, and started to drink with them. She kept saying she had all the money in the house and must really go off and do the shopping, but all the Reillys had a remarkable capacity for reminding themselves of what they should be doing without doing it, and what began as a protest ended up as a turn. The fellows said she was a great card. When she came home half tight with only half the shopping done Brigid smacked her face.

Evelyn knew she ought to kill Brigid, but she didn't do that either. Instead she went to her room and wept. Jim came up later to go to Midnight Mass with her. He was a bit lit up too but drink only gave Jim words without warmth. It roused his sense of abstract justice, and instead of soothing Evelyn as he should have done he set out to prove to her how unreasonable she was.

'My goodness,' he said with a feeble oratorical gesture, 'what do you expect? Here's poor Brigid trying to get things ready for Christmas and you drinking yourself stupid down in Johnny Desmond's with Casserley and Doyle and Maurice the Slug. Sure, of course, she was mad.'

'That's right,' Evelyn said, beginning to flame. 'It's all my fault as usual.'

'There's nothing usual about it,' Jim went on with futile reasonableness, 'only you don't know what a good sister you have. The girl was a mother to you. A mother! I only wish I had a mother like her.'

'You have time still,' said Evelyn, beside herself.

'I wouldn't be good enough for her,' said Jim with sickly servility.

'If you're not good enough for her you're not good enough for me.'

'I never said I was. Are you going to make it up and come to Mass?'

'Go to hell!' snapped Evelyn.

All through the holidays she brooded over him and over her own weak character and rotten luck, and the day after the holidays, in the mood of disillusionment that follows Christmas, while still feeling that no one in the world gave a damn for her, she took out Jim's savings and caught the boat for London. The Reillys had friends there; a disorderly family called Ronan who had once lived on the terrace and had to get out of it in a hurry.

This was a scandal, if you like! The only one who really had a tolerant word to say for Evelyn was Joan, who said that, though, of course, it was wrong of Evelyn to have stolen the money, running away was the only decent way out of an impossible marriage. But then, Joan, as well as disliking Jim, loved romance and excitement. In Brigid the romantic was subdued a little by the mother; she knew it would be her responsibility to get Joan off her father's hands and that it had all been made ten times more difficult by the reports that were now going round that the Reilly girls were really what the schoolboys' mothers had always proclaimed them to be.

As for Myles, he was brokenhearted, or as near broken-hearted as his temperament permitted him to be. 'The one decent boy that ever came to the house,' he said with his face in his hands, 'and he had to be robbed, and robbed by a daughter of mine. God, Bridgie, isn't it cruel?' After that he began to cry quietly to himself. 'I loved that boy: I loved him as if he was my own son. I could have spent my last days happily with him. And the little house I was going to build for him and all — everything gone!' Then he beat the wall with his fists and cried: 'God, if only I could lay my hands on her I'd strangle her! Evelyn, Evelyn, you were the last I thought would shame me.'

Jim took it as you'd expect a fellow like that to take it. The person he seemed most concerned about was Myles. When he took Myles out for a drink, the old boy sat with the tears in his eyes and then spread out his big paws like claws and silently closed them round the spot where he imagined his daughter's neck to be.

'That's what I'd like to do to her, Jim,' he said.

'Ah, you're not still chewing over that!' Jim said reproachfully.

Myles closed his eyes and shook his head.

'What the hell else can I do?' he asked, almost sobbing. 'It's not the money, Jim; it's not the money, boy. I'll pay that back.'

'You'll do nothing of the sort,' Jim said quietly. 'That's a matter between Evelyn and me. It has nothing to do with you.'

'No, no, it's my responsibility, my responsibility entirely, Jim,' cried Myles in agony, swaying to and fro. He was indignant at the very suggestion that he wasn't responsible; if he'd had it he would have paid it ten times over sooner than carry the burden of it on his mind. But Jim knew his capacity for discussing what was the right thing to do without doing it, and indeed, without any prospect of doing it. Within a few weeks it had boiled down to the skilled assistance Jim would receive in any house he built for the girl who replaced Evelyn. But Jim showed no signs of even wanting to replace her. For months he was drinking more than he should have been.

2

Then, when all the commotion had died away, when Jim ceased to go to the Reillys' and there was no longer even a question of the ninety pounds being paid back, Evelyn came home. There was no nonsense about her slinking in the back door in the early hours of the morning. She wore a grand new tailor-made with a hat like a hoop and arrived at the house in a car. Brigid watched her pay off the driver, and her face looked old and grim.

'I suppose that was the last of the money?' she asked bitterly.

'What money?' Evelyn asked, on the defensive at once.

'Why? Did you rob some other man as well?' Brigid asked. 'What money, indeed?'

'That's gone long ago,' Evelyn said haughtily. 'I'm paying it back. I suppose I can get a job, can't I?'

'I suppose so,' said Brigid. 'If Jim Piper will give you a character.'

Myles got up and stumped upstairs to his room. He was very agitated. He told Brigid that he'd kill Evelyn with his own two hands, and became still more agitated when Brigid told him sharply that it would be better if he used a stick. He told Brigid that he didn't like being spoken to in that way. He didn't either. The truth was that Myles was in a very difficult position. Ever since Evelyn's fall Brigid had developed a high moral tone which was far too like her mother's to be wholesome. Unlike her mother's it could not be short-circuited by blandishments or embraces or even softened by tears. The girl wanted him to keep regular hours; she wanted him, suffering as he was from cruel responsibilities, to deny himself the consolation of a friendly chat after his day's work. There was a hard streak in Brigid; she never realized the strain he was living under.

For all her faults, no one could say that of Evelyn. She might be weak and a thief and deserve strangling, but she always knew the proper tone to adopt to a father a bit the worse for drink who knew he had done wrong and didn't want to be reminded of it. He knew he had sworn that she should never set

foot in the house again, but damn it, she was his daughter, and
– though it was something he wouldn't like to say – he was glad
to see her home.

Joan too was glad, and she showed it. She was doing a tearing line with a bank clerk, a gorgeous fellow of violent passions,
and Brigid, regardless of the way she had behaved herself with
Ben Hennessy, chaperoned her like mad. Brigid herself had
contracted a regular, a draper caller Considine, and drapers
being exceedingly respectable, she was taking no more chances.
The Reillys were to be respectable if it killed them. Again and
again with her cutting tongue she made it plain that Evelyn
wasn't wanted. Joan thought it disgusting.

Besides, Evelyn's descriptions of life in London were a revelation to her. It seemed that in disgust with herself and life she
had begun a sordid and idiotic love affair, and used it merely to
lacerate herself further. It was only when she realized that the
man she was associating with despised her almost as much as
she despised herself that she broke it off and came home. Joan
put this down to her sister's unfortunate character and her inability to get the best out of life. In Evelyn's position she would
have acted quite differently. She wouldn't have permitted any
man to despise her; she would certainly not have despised herself, and under no circumstances would she have come home.
It worked so much on Joan's imagination that she even thought
of going away, just to show Evelyn how it should be done.

But there was still one thing Evelyn had to reckon with. She
had to face Jim. This is one of the tests which the small town
imposes, which cannot be avoided and cannot really be worked
out in advance. One evening late when she was coming home
from a friend's she ran into Jim. There was no getting out of
it. He was taken aback though he tried not to show it. He raised
his cap and stopped. Evelyn stopped too. When it came to the
test she found she couldn't walk past him; she was a girl of
weak character.

'Hullo, Evelyn,' he said in a tone of surprise.

'Hullo,' she replied chokingly.

'Back for a holiday?' he asked – as if he didn't know!

'No, for good.'

'Homesick?' he added, still trying to make talk.

'Ah, for God's sake,' she cried with sudden violence, 'if you want to talk, come away where we won't have the whole town looking at us.'

She led the way, walking fast and silently, full of suppressed anger and humiliation. Jim loped along beside her, his hands in the pockets of his trench coat. She turned up Lovers' Lane, a place they had used in their courting days. It was a long, dark, winding boreen with high walls, between two estates. Then she turned on him, at bay.

It is extraordinary what women can do in self-defence. She shouted at him. She said it was all his fault for being such a doormat; that no one with a spark of manliness in him could have let her be treated as she was at home, and that he knew she was heart-scalded and hadn't the spirit to stand up for her. She all but implied that it was he who had pinched her savings. He didn't try to interrupt her.

'Well,' he said lamely when she had talked herself out, 'it's no use crying over spilt milk.'

'Oh, if it was only milk!' she said and began to cry. 'Ronan's is no better than a kip. I never meant to take your money. I meant to get a job and send it back to you, but they kept cadging and cadging until every penny was gone.'

'I suppose we can be thankful it was no worse,' he said, and then held out his hand. 'Anyway, are we quits now?'

She threw her arms about him and squeezed him fiercely. She was weeping hysterically and he patted her back gently, talking to her in a low, soothing voice. She did not tell him about the fellow in London. She wanted to forget it, for it made her ashamed every time she thought of it. Besides, she couldn't see that it was any business of Jim's.

After that night they continued to meet, but in a peculiar way, unknown to their families. Both were self-conscious about it. Evelyn would not invite Jim to the house and he was too proud to invite himself. The truth was that she felt Jim was behaving with his usual lack of manliness. He should have cut her dead when they met or, failing that, should have got drunk and beaten her up, all the more because she had behaved so badly in London. The fact that she hadn't told him of what took place in London only made his conduct more indefensible, and she suffered almost as much on his account as if the fault had been her own. They met after dark in out-of-the-way places, and it was weeks before word got round that they were walking out again. Joan was bitterly disappointed; she had thought better of Evelyn. Brigid, seeing a grand chance of washing out the scandal of the stolen money, changed her tune and demanded that Jim should see her sister at the house, but Evelyn refused sulkily. By this time her main anxiety was to keep Jim and Joan apart so that the London scandal mightn't leak out: not that she thought Joan would wish to betray her but because for some reason she was enormously proud of Evelyn's conduct and would be bound to boast of it. That was the worst of a romantic sister.

'If you're going to marry Jim Piper it's only right,' said Brigid.

'Jim Piper didn't say he wanted to marry me,' said Evelyn.

'Then what are ye walking out for?' cried Brigid.

'What do people usually walk out for?' Evelyn asked scornfully.

It was months before Brigid realized why Evelyn was so stubborn about not inviting Jim to the house, and by that time it was too late. Joan knew but Joan wouldn't tell. Evelyn told Jim one summer evening at the edge of a wood. She did it with an air of boyish toughness and braggadocio, smoking a cigarette. Jim was aghast.

'Are you sure, Evvie?' he asked mildly.

'Certain,' said Evelyn. 'Joan looked it up in the library.'

Jim gave a bitter, embarrassed laugh and lay back with his hands under his head.

'That's a bit of a shock all right,' he said. 'What are we going to do about it?'

'I suppose I'll only have to go back to Ronan's,' Evelyn said lightly. 'They won't mind. What would shock them would sweat a black.'

'I suppose so,' Jim said ruefully. 'We can't afford to rush into anything now.'

'No one is trying to rush you into anything,' she said hotly. 'Get that out of your head.'

She was silent for a moment; then she got up quickly, brushed her skirt and crossed the fence into the lane. Jim came after her with a hangdog air. As he jumped down she turned and faced him, all ablaze.

'Don't attempt to follow me!' she cried.

'Why not?' he asked in surprise.

'Why not?' she repeated mockingly. 'As if you didn't know! Oh, you codded me nicely! You wanted to get your own back for the money and you did, if that's any satisfaction to you.'

'It's no satisfaction at all to me,' Jim said, raising his voice. There was a queer, unhappy doggedness about his air. He put his hands in his trouser pockets and stood with his legs wide. His voice lacked resonance. 'And I wasn't trying to get my own back for anything, though I had plenty of cause.'

'You had; you and your old money; I wish I never saw it.'

'It's not the money.'

'Then what is it?'

He didn't reply. He had no need to. Under his accusing eyes she reddened again. It had never crossed her mind that he might know.

'I suppose Joan was chattering,' she said bitterly.

'Nobody was chattering at all,' he said scornfully. 'I knew all about it from the first night I saw you. You couldn't conceal it.'

'I wasn't trying to conceal it,' she blazed. 'I have nothing to hide from you.'

'I'm not throwing it up at you,' he protested. 'I'll marry you just the same when I can.'

'Marry me?' she spat. 'I wouldn't marry you if you were the last living thing left in the world – you worm!'

Then she strode off down the lane, humiliated to the very depth of her being. If she had gone away without saying anything to him she could have kept her pride, but she knew that in her desperation she had as good as asked him to marry her and, what was worse, asked him under false pretences. This was not what she had intended when she shut up about the

London affair; then her only idea had been to protect her own wounded sensibilities, but now she realized that if ever the story got round, she would appear no better than any other little tart, pretending to be innocent so as to kid a man into marrying her. Nothing she could now do would alter that interpretation. She went home in such a fury of rage and misery that she blurted it out in a few sentences to Brigid.

'You'd better get some money for me somewhere. I'm going to have a kid, and I'll have to go to London to have it.'

'You're going to—?' began Brigid, growing pale.

'Have a kid, I said,' shouted Evelyn savagely.

'Is it Jim Piper?'

'Never mind!'

'He'll have to marry you.'

'He won't. I asked him and he told me to go to hell.'

'We'll soon see about that.'

'You won't. I did the same thing with another fellow in London and he found out.'

'You – so that's what you were up to in London.'

'That's what I was up to,' sneered Evelyn. 'Anyway, I wouldn't marry that fellow now if he came to me on his knees.'

Then she went to bed and Joan, for once a little-awed, brought up her tea. Myles first wept and then went out and got drunk. He said if it was anyone else he'd go out at once and kill him with his own two hands, but a fellow who had had his savings stolen on him! That was the real tragedy of being poor, that it destroyed a man's self-respect and made it impossible for him to wipe out his humiliations in blood. *Blood*, that was what he wanted. But Brigid didn't want anyone's blood. She wanted to marry Considine, the draper, and though Considine was broadminded enough as drapers go, she didn't want to give him anything more to be broadminded about. She stormed out to interview Jim's mother.

With all her responsibilities, Brigid was still something of a child. Standing with one hand on the table and the other on her hip, Mrs Piper dominated the scene from the first moment. She asked in the most ingenuous way in the world how such a thing could happen in a well-conducted house, and when Brigid assured her that it hadn't happened there Mrs Piper said wasn't it lucky that Evelyn didn't get pneumonia as well. Brigid has as much chance against her as an innocent naked savage against a machine-gun post.

While they were arguing Jim came in and hung up his cap.

'You know what I came about, Jim,' Brigid said challengingly.

'If I don't I can guess, Brigid,' he replied with a tight smile.

'The girl has no mother.'

'She has something as good, Brigid,' Jim replied simply, and Brigid suddenly realized that his respect for her was something he did not put off and on as it suited him. It gave her new dignity and confidence.

'You'll marry her for my sake, Jim?' she asked.

'I'll marry her the minute I'm able, Brigid,' he said stubbornly, putting his hands in his trouser pockets, a trick he had to give him the feeling of stability. 'I may be able to marry her in a year's time, but I can't do it now.'

'A year's time will be too late, Jim,' Brigid cried. 'A girl in her position can afford to do without a house but she can't do without a husband.'

'And start off in furnished rooms with a kid?' Jim replied scornfully. 'I saw too many do that, and I never saw one that came to any good.'

Brigid looked at him doubtfully. She didn't believe him; she felt he was holding out on her only because of his bitterness about Evelyn's betrayal. It caused her to make a false move.

'I know she behaved like a bitch about that fellow in London,' she said. 'I only heard it today for the first time. But surely, seeing the state she's in, you're big enough to forgive her.'

The look on Jim's face convinced her that she was right. His expression showed pain, humiliation, and bewilderment, but his voice remained firm.

'If I didn't forgive her I wouldn't be in the fix I'm in now,' he said.

'What's that?' his mother cried. 'What's that about a fellow in London? So that's what she was up to, the vagabond! And now she's trying to put the blame on my innocent boy!'

'She's not trying to put the blame on anybody,' Jim said with the first sign of real anger he had shown. 'I'm responsible, and I'm not denying it, but I can't marry her now. She'll have to go to London.'

'But we haven't the money to send her to London,' Brigid cried in exasperation. 'Don't you know well the way we're situated?'

'I'll pay my share,' Jim said. 'And I'll pay for the kid, but I won't do any more.'

'Leave her pay for it out of what she stole!' hissed his mother. 'Oh, my, that many a fine family was reared on less!'

'I'm going straight up to Father Ring,' Brigid said desperately.

'You can spare yourself the trouble,' said Jim flatly. 'Ring isn't going to make me marry Evelyn, nor anyone else either.'

This was strong language from a young fellow of Jim's age, but it was no more than Father Ring himself expected.

'Brigid,' he said, squeezing the girl's arm sympathetically, 'I'll do what I can but I wouldn't have much hope. To tell you the truth I never expected better. The best thing I can do is to see Lane.'

So off he went to interview Jim's employer, Mick Lane, at his own home.

'You could warn him he'd get the sack if he didn't marry her,' he suggested.

'Oh, begod, Father, I could not,' replied Lane in alarm. 'I wouldn't mind anyone else, but Jim is the sort of fellow would walk out the door on me if he thought I was threatening him, and I'd be a hell of a long time getting as good a man. I might talk to him myself in a friendly way.'

'Mick,' said Father Ring in a disappointment, 'you'd only be wasting your time. Is it a fellow that wouldn't sing at a parish concert without a fee? It might be the best thing for the poor girl in the long run.'

3

Next time Evelyn came back from London without any finery; the baby was put out to nurse up the country and not referred to again. It caused a lot of talk. There were plenty to say that Jim was in the wrong, that, even allowing that the girl was damaged goods, a fellow might swallow his pride. Better men had had to do it. But Jim in his quiet, stubborn way went on as though he didn't even know there was talk.

Ultimately, it did the Reillys no great harm, because Joan became engaged to the gorgeous passionate fellow at the bank and Brigid married Considine. Evelyn set her teeth and stuck it out. She went twice to see Owen, her baby, but gave it up when she realized that you can't retain a child's affection by visiting him two or three times a year.

For months she didn't see Jim. Then one evening when she went for a walk in the country, she came on him about a mile out of town, studying the wreck of a car which he was trying to make something of. It was one of those occasions when any-one is at a disadvantage; when it depends on the weather or your digestion – or, going further back, what sort your parents were – what you do. Evelyn was her father's daughter and, having no true feminine pride to direct her, she naturally did the wrong thing.

'Hello,' she said.

'Oh, hello, Evelyn,' Jim said, raising his cap. 'How are you getting on?'

'All right,' she replied curtly, with the sinking of the heart she would have felt anyhow, knowing that the decision of a lifetime had been taken, and that, as usual, it was the wrong one.

'Can I give you a lift?'

'I wasn't going anywhere in particular,' she said, realizing the enormous effort of will it would take to restore the situation to what it had been a moment before.

That night, crazy with rage, she wrote him a blistering letter, asking how he had dared to speak to her and warning him that if he did it again she would slap his face. Then, remembering the lonesome evening she would spend if she posted it, she put it in her bag and went off to meet him. While they were sitting on a gate up a country lane she realized that now she would never send the letter, and the thought of it in her bag irritated her. It was as though she saw the two women in her fighting for mastery. She took it out and tore it up.

'What's that?' asked Jim.

'A letter to you.'

'Can't I see it?'

'You'd hate it.'

That extraordinary man threw back his head and laughed like a kid. There was no doubt about it, he was a worm, but at any rate he was her worm; he didn't divide his attentions, and even if she didn't think much of him, there was no one else she thought more of. She couldn't merely sit at home, waiting for someone who'd overlook her past. Fellows in Ireland were death on girls' pasts.

But now the sense of guilt was ingrained: when she met Jim in town she merely saluted him, and if she had anyone with her she tried to avoid doing even that. It was funny, but she felt if she stopped to speak to him she would suddenly be overcome by the popular feeling and tear his eyes out. It was again that feeling that she was really two women and didn't know which of them she wanted to be.

As a result it was months before people knew they were walking out again. This time there was a thundering row and the Reillys were the most scandalized of all. Even Joan deserted her. It was all very well for Brigid, who had her draper where he couldn't escape, but Joan's bank clerk was still a toss-up and everyone knew the unmannerly way the banks had of prying into their officials' business.

'Honest to God,' Joan said contemptuously, 'you haven't a spark of pride or decency.'

'Well, neither has he, so we're well matched,' Evelyn said despondently.

'God knows, 'tis a pity to spoil two houses with ye.'

'It's all very well for you, Joan,' said Evelyn, 'but I have the kid's future to think of.'

This wasn't true; it was a long time since Evelyn had thought of Owen's future because it was only too plain that he had none, but it was the best excuse she could think of.

'You'd hate him to be an only child,' snapped Joan.

'I'm not such a fool,' said Evelyn, deeply hurt.

'Fool is the word,' retorted Joan.

Her father ignored her presence in the house. The latest scandal was the final touch. He was disappointed in Evelyn but he was far more disappointed in Jim, who had once shown signs of character. Up to this he had felt it was only daughters who threatened a man's peace of mind; now he began to think a son might be as bad.

When Joan married it made things easier for him, though not for Evelyn. It is always a lonesome thing for a girl when the last of her sisters has gone and the prams have begun to come back. It was worse on her because she had never pushed her own pram, and the babies she fussed over were getting something her own would never get. It fixed and confirmed her feeling of inferiority to Brigid and Joan, almost as though she had done it deliberately. She sometimes wondered whether she hadn't.

But it gradually dawned on her father that if God had tried to reward him for a well-spent life with a secure old age, He couldn't well have planned anything more satisfactory than a more or less unmarriageable daughter who could never take a high moral line. If he came in drunk every night of the week and cut her down on the housekeeping, her sins would still outnumber his. A man like Myles in such as unassailable position of moral superiority could not help being kind. 'God's truth,' he muttered to his cronies, 'I can't blame the girl. I'm as bad myself. It's a thing you can't talk about, but since the missis died I had my own temptations.' Sometimes when he saw her getting ready to go out and see Jim Piper he patted her on the shoulder, mumbled a few words of encouragement, and went out with his eyes wet. Myles was like that, a man of no character!

4

One evening while he and Evelyn were having their tea the latch was lifted and Jim Piper himself walked in. It was his first visit since the far-away night when he had called to console Myles for his daughter's crime.

'God save all here,' he said and beamed at them with unusual magnanimity.

Myles looked up, drew a deep breath through his nose and looked away. It was all damn well condoning his daughter's misbehaviour, but he refused to condone Jim's. Even Evelyn was embarrassed and cross. It wasn't like Jim.

'Hello,' she replied with no great warmth. 'What do you want?'

'Oh, just a few words with you,' Jim replied cheerfully, placing a chair for himself in the middle of the kitchen. 'Nothing important. Don't interrupt yourself. Finish your supper. If you have a paper I could look at it.'

'There you are,' she said, mystified, but no newspaper was capable of halting Jim's unusual flow of garrulity.

'Good evening, Mr Reilly,' he said to her father, and then as Myles ignored him he threw back his head and laughed. 'I don't know what's coming over Irish hospitality,' he added with a touch of indignation. 'You pass the time of day to a man and he won't even answer. Begod,' he added with growing scorn, 'they won't even ask you to sit down. Go on with their tea overright you, and not ask have you a mouth on you! "What do you want?"' he echoed Evelyn.

She realized in a flash what was the matter with him. He was drunk. She had never seen him so bad before, and he was not the type which gets drunk gracefully. He was too angular for that. He threw his limbs about in a dislocated way like a rag doll. All the same it put her at her ease. She was always more comfortable with men like that.

'Far from tea you were today, wherever you were,' she said, fetching a cup and saucer. 'Do you want tea?'

'Oh, no,' said Jim bitterly with another dislocated motion of his arm. 'I'm only making conversation. I didn't have a bit to eat since morning and then I'm asked if I want tea!'

'You'd better have something to eat so,' she said. 'Will you have sausages?'

'Isn't it about time you asked me?' Jim asked with grave reproach, looking at her owlishly.

It was only with the greatest difficulty that she kept from laughing outright. But her father, who had recognized Jim's condition from the start, had the toper's sensitiveness. He drew a deep breath through his nose, banged his fist on the table, and exploded in a 'Christ! In my own house!' Then he got up, went upstairs and slammed the bedroom door behind him. No doubt he was resisting the temptation to kill Jim with his own hands. Jim laughed. Apparently he had no notion of his peril.

'Call him back,' he said, tossing his head.

'Why?'

'I want to ask him to my wedding.'

'Go on!' she said with amusement. 'Are you getting married?'

'I can't stand this bloody bachelor life,' Jim said pathetically.

'So I noticed,' she said. 'Who's the doll?'

'One moment, please!' he said severely. 'We're coming to that. First, I have a crow to pluck with you.'

'Go on!' she said, her smile fading. People always seemed to have crows to pluck with Evelyn, and she was getting tired of it.

'You said you wouldn't marry me if I was the last living thing in the world,' he said, wagging his finger sternly at her. 'I'm not a man to bear malice but I'm entitled to remind you of what you said. As well as that, you said I was a worm. I'm not complaining about that either. All I'm doing is asking are you prepared – prepared to withdraw those statements?' he finished up successfully.

'You never know,' she said, her lip beginning to quiver. 'You might ask me again some time you're sober.'

'You think I don't know what I'm saying?' he asked triumphantly as he rose to his feet – but he rose unsteadily.

'Do you?' she asked.

'I banked the last two hundred quid today,' said Jim in the same tone. 'Two hundred quid and five for Ring, and if that's not enough for the old bastard I'll soon find someone that will be glad of it. I drank the rest. You can go down the country now, tomorrow if you like, and bring Owen back, and tell the whole bloody town to kiss your ass. Now, do I know what I'm saying?' he shouted with the laughter bubbling up through his words.

It was a great pity he couldn't remain steady. But Evelyn no longer noticed that. She only noticed the laughter and triumph and realized how much of Jim's life she had wasted along with her own. She gave a low cry and ran upstairs after her father. Jim looked after her dazedly and collapsed with another dislocated gesture. It was useless trying to carry on a discussion with an unstable family like the Reillys who kept running up and down stairs the whole time.

It was her father's turn now. He stumped heavily down the stairs, gripping the banisters with both hands as though he were about to spring, and then stood at the foot. This time it was clear that Jim's hour had come. He didn't mind. He knew he was going to be sick anyway.

'What's wrong with that girl?' Myles asked in a shaking voice.

'I don't know,' Jim said despondently, tossing the limp wet hair back from his forehead. 'Waiting, I suppose.'

'Waiting?' Myles asked. 'Waiting for what?'

'This,' shouted Jim, waving his arm wildly and letting it collapse by his side. 'The money is there now. Two hundred quid, and five for the priest. You start work on that house at eight tomorrow morning. See?'

Myles took a few moments to digest this. Even for a man of expansive nature, from murder to marriage is a bit of a leap. He stroked his chin and looked at Jim, lying there with his head hanging and one arm dead by his side. He chuckled. Such a story! Christ, such a story!

'And not a drop of drink in the house!' he exclaimed. 'Evelyn!' he called up the stairs.

There was no reply.

'Evelyn!' he repeated peremptorily, as though he were a man accustomed to instant obedience. 'We'll let her alone for a while,' he mumbled, scratching his head. 'I suppose it came as a bit of shock to her. She's a good girl, Jim, a fine girl. You're making no mistake. Take it from me.' But even in that state, Jim, he realized, was not the sort to need encouragement, and he beamed and rubbed his hands. For more than anything else in the world Myles loved a man, a *man*. He stood looking fondly down on his semi-conscious son-in-law.

'You thundering ruffian!' he chuckled, shaking his head. 'Oh, God, if only I might have done it thirty years ago I'd be a made man today.'

The Luceys

It's extraordinary, the bitterness there can be in a town like ours between two people of the same family. More particularly between two people of the same family. I suppose living more or less in public as we do we are either killed or cured by it, and the same communal sense that will make a man be battered into a reconciliation he doesn't feel gives added importance to whatever quarrel he thinks must not be composed. God knows, most of the time you'd be more sorry for a man like that than anything else.

The Luceys were like that. There were two brothers, Tom and Ben, and there must have been a time when the likeness between them was greater than the difference, but that was long before most of us knew them. Tom was the elder; he came in for the drapery shop. Ben had to have a job made for him on the County Council. This was the first difference and it grew and grew. Both were men of intelligence and education but Tom took it more seriously. As Ben said with a grin, he could damn well afford to with the business behind him.

It was an old-fashioned shop which prided itself on only stocking the best, and though the prices were high and Tom in his irascible opinionated way refused to abate them – he said haggling was degrading! – a lot of farmers' wives would still go nowhere else. Ben listened to his brother's high notions with his eyes twinkling, rather as he read the books which came his way, with profound respect and the feeling that this would all be grand for some other place, but was entirely inapplicable to the affairs of the County Council. God alone would ever be able to disentangle these, and meanwhile the only course open to a prudent man was to keep his mind to himself. If Tom didn't like the way the County Council was run, neither did

Ben, but that was the way things were, and it rather amused him to rub it in to his virtuous brother.

Tom and Ben were both married. Tom's boy, Peter, was the great friend of his cousin, Charlie – called 'Charliss' by his Uncle Tom. They were nice boys; Peter a fat, heavy, handsome lad who blushed whenever a stranger spoke to him, and Charles with a broad face that never blushed at anything. The two families were always friendly; the mothers liked to get together over a glass of port wine and discuss the fundamental things that made the Lucey brothers not two inexplicable characters but two aspects of one inexplicable family character; the brothers enjoyed their regular chats about the way the world was going, for intelligent men are rare and each appreciated the other's shrewdness.

Only young Charlie was occasionally mystified by his Uncle Tom; he hated calling for Peter unless he was sure his uncle was out, for otherwise he might be sent into the front room to talk to him. The front room alone was enough to upset any high-spirited lad, with its thick carpet, mahogany sideboard, ornamental clock, and gilt mirror with cupids. The red curtains alone would depress you, and as well as these there was a glass-fronted mahogany bookcase the length of one wall, with books in sets, too big for anyone only a priest to read: *The History of Ireland, The History of the Popes, The Roman Empire, The Life of Johnson,* and *The Cabinet of Literature.* It gave Charlie the same sort of shivers as the priest's front room. His uncle suited it, a small, frail man, dressed in clerical black with a long pinched yellow face, tight lips, a narrow skull going bald up the brow, and a pair of tin specs.

All conversations with his uncle tended to stick in Charlie's mind for the simple but alarming reason that he never understood what the hell they were about, but one conversation in particular haunted him for years as showing the dangerous state of lunacy to which a man could be reduced by reading old books. Charlie was no fool, far from it; but low cunning and the most genuine benevolence were mixed in him in almost equal parts, producing a blend that was not without charm but gave no room for subtlety or irony.

'Good afternoon, Charliss,' said his uncle after Charlie had tied what he called 'the ould pup' to the leg of the hallstand. 'How are you?'

'All right,' Charlie said guardedly. (He hated being called Charliss; it made him sound such a sissy.)

'Take a seat, Charliss,' said his uncle benevolently. 'Peter will be down in a minute.'

'I won't,' said Charlie. 'I'd be afraid of the ould pup.'

'The expression, Charliss,' said his uncle in that rasping little voice of his, 'sounds like a contradiction in terms, but, not being familiar with dogs, I presume 'tis correct.'

'Ah, 'tis,' said Charlie, just to put the old man's mind at rest.

'And how is your father, Charliss?'

'His ould belly is bad again,' said Charlie. 'He'd be all right only the ould belly plays hell with him.'

'I'm sorry to hear it,' his uncle said gravely. 'And tell me, Charliss,' he added, cocking his head on one side like a bird, 'what is he saying about me now?'

This was one of the dirtiest of his Uncle Tom's tricks, assuming that Charlie's father was saying things about him, which to give Ben his due, he usually was. But on the other hand, he was admitted to be one of the smartest men in town, so he was entitled to do so, while everyone without exception appeared to agree that his uncle had a slate loose. Charlie looked at him cautiously, low cunning struggling with benevolence in him, for his uncle though queer was open-handed, and you wouldn't want to offend him. Benevolence won.

'He's saying if you don't mind yourself you'll end up in the poorhouse,' he said with some notion that if only his uncle knew the things people said about him he might mend his ways.

'Your father is right as always, Charliss,' said his uncle, rising and standing on the hearth with his hands behind his back and his little legs well apart. 'Your father is perfectly right. There are two main classes of people, Charliss – those who gravitate towards the poorhouse and those who gravitate towards the jail ... Do you know what "gravitate" means, Charliss?'

'I do not,' said Charlie without undue depression. It struck him as being an unlikely sort of word.

' "Gravitate", Charliss, means "tend" or "incline". Don't tell me you don't know what they mean!'

'I don't,' said Charlie.

'Well, do you know what this is?' his uncle asked smilingly as he held up a coin.

'I do,' said Charlie, humouring him as he saw that the conversation was at last getting somewhere. 'A tanner.'

'I am not familiar with the expression, Charliss,' his uncle said tartly and Charlie knew, whatever he'd said out of the way, his uncle was so irritated that he was liable to put the tanner back. 'We'll call it sixpence. Your eyes, I notice, gravitate towards the sixpence,' (Charlie was so shocked that his eyes instantly gravitated towards his uncle) 'and in the same way, people gravitate, or turn naturally, towards the jail or poorhouse. Only a small number of either group reach their destination, though – which might be just as well for myself and your father,' he added in a low impressive voice, swaying forward and tightening his lips. 'Do you understand a word I'm saying, Charliss?' he added with a charming smile.

'I do not,' said Charlie.

'Good man! Good man!' his uncle said approvingly. 'I admire an honest and manly spirit in anybody. Don't forget your sixpence, Charliss.'

And as he went off with Peter, Charlie scowled and muttered savagely under his breath: 'Mod! Mod! Mod! The bleddy mon is mod!'

2

When the boys grew up Peter trained for a solicitor while Charlie, one of a large family, followed his father into the County Council. He grew up a very handsome fellow with a square, solemn, dark-skinned face, a thick red lower lip, and a mass of curly black hair. He was reputed to be a great man with greyhounds and girls and about as dependable with one as with the others. His enemies called him 'a crooked bloody bastard' and his father, a shrewd man, noted with alarm that Charlie thought him simpleminded.

The two boys continued the best of friends, though Peter, with an office in Asragh, moved in circles where Charlie felt himself lost; professional men whose status was calculated on their furniture and food and wine. Charlie thought that sort of entertainment a great pity. A man could have all the fun he wanted out of life without wasting his time on expensive and unsatisfactory meals and carrying on polite conversation while you dodged between bloody little tables that were always falling over, but Charlie, who was a modest lad, admired the way Peter never knocked anything over and never said: 'Chrisht!' Wine, coffee-cups, and talk about old books came as easy to him as talk about a dog or a horse.

Charlie was thunderstruck when the news came to him that Peter was in trouble. He heard it first from Mackesy the detective, whom he hailed outside the courthouse. (Charlie was like his father in that; he couldn't let a man go by without a greeting.)

'Hullo, Matt,' he shouted gaily from the courthouse steps. 'Is it myself or my father you're after?'

'I'll let ye off for today,' said Mackesy, making a garden seat of the crossbar of his bicycle. Then he lowered his voice so that it didn't travel farther than Charlie. 'I wouldn't mind having a word with a relative of yours, though.'

'A what, Matt?' Charlie asked, skipping down the steps on the scent of news. (He was like his father in that, too.) 'You don't mean one of the Luceys is after forgetting himself?'

'Then you didn't hear about Peter?'

'Peter! Peter in trouble! You're not serious, Matt?'

'There's a lot of his clients would be glad if I wasn't, Cha,' Mackesy said grimly. 'I thought you'd know about it as ye were such pals.'

'But we are, man, we are,' Charlie insisted. 'Sure, wasn't I at the dogs with him – when was it? – last Thursday? I never noticed a bloody thing, though, now you mention it, he was lashing pound notes on that Cloonbullogue dog. I told him the Dalys could never train a dog.'

Charlie left Mackesy, his mind in a whirl. He tore through the cashier's office. His father was sitting at his desk, signing paying-orders. He was wearing a grey tweed cap, a grey tweed suit, and a brown cardigan. He was a stocky, powerfully built man with a great expanse of chest, a plump, dark, hairy face, long quizzical eyes that tended to close in slits; hair in his nose, hair in his ears; hair on his high cheekbones that made them like small cabbage-patches.

He made no comment on Charlie's news, but stroked his chin and looked worried. Then Charlie shot out to see his uncle. Quill, the assistant, was serving in the shop and Charlie stumped in behind the counter to the fitting-room. His uncle had been looking out the back, all crumpled up. When Charlie came in he pulled himself erect with fictitious jauntiness. With his old black coat and wrinkled yellow face he had begun to look like an old rabbi.

'What's this I hear about Peter?' began Charlie, who was never one to be ceremonious.

'Bad news travels fast, Charlie,' said his uncle in his dry little voice, clamping his lips so tightly that the wrinkles ran up his cheeks from the corners of his mouth. He was so upset that he forgot even to say 'Charliss'.

'Have you any notion how much it is?' asked Charlie.

'I have not, Charlie,' Tom said bitterly. 'I need hardly say my son did not take me into his confidence about the extent of his robberies.'

'And what are you going to do?'

'What can I do?' The lines of pain belied the harsh little staccato that broke up every sentence into disjointed phrases as if it were a political speech. 'You saw yourself, Charliss, the way I reared that boy. You saw the education I gave him. I gave him the thing I was denied myself, Charliss. I gave him an honourable profession. And now for the first time in my life I am ashamed to show my face in my own shop. What can I do?'

'Ah, now, ah, now, Uncle Tom, we know all that,' Charlie said truculently, 'but that's not going to get us anywhere. What can we do now?'

'Is it true that Peter took money that was entrusted to him?' Tom asked oratorically.

'To be sure he did,' replied Charlie without the thrill of horror which his uncle seemed to expect. 'I do it myself every month, only I put it back.'

'And is it true he ran away from his punishment instead of standing his ground like a man?' asked Tom, paying no attention to him.

'What the hell else would he do?' asked Charlie, who entirely failed to appreciate the spiritual beauty of atonement. 'Begod, if I had two years' hard labour facing me you wouldn't see my heels for dust.'

'I dare say you think I'm old-fashioned, Charliss,' said his uncle, 'but that's not the way I was reared, nor the way my son was reared.'

'And that's where the ferryboat left ye,' snorted Charlie. 'Now that sort of thing may be all very well, Uncle Tom, but 'tis no use taking it to the fair. Peter made some mistake, the way we all make mistakes, but instead of coming to me or some other friend, he lost his nerve and started gambling. Chrisht, didn't I see it happen to better men? You don't know how much it is?'

'No, Charliss, I don't.'

'Do you know where he is, even?'

'His mother knows.'

'I'll talk to my old fellow. We might be able to do something. If the bloody fool might have told me on Thursday instead of backing that Cloonbullogue dog!'

Charlie returned to the office to find his father sitting at his desk with his hands joined and his pipe in his mouth, staring nervously at the door.

'Well?'

'We'll go over to Asragh and talk to Toolan of the Guards ourselves,' said Charlie. 'I want to find out how much he let himself in for. We might even get a look at the books.'

'Can't his father do it?' Ben asked gloomily.

'Do you think he'd understand them?'

'Well, he was always fond of literature,' Ben said shortly.

'God help him,' said Charlie. 'He has enough of it now.'

''Tis all his own conceit,' Ben said angrily, striding up and down the office with his hands in his trouser pockets. 'He was always good at criticizing other people. Even when you got in here it was all influence. Of course, he'd never use influence. Now he wants us to use it.'

'That's all very well,' Charlie said reasonably, 'but this is no time for raking up old scores.'

'Who's raking up old scores?' his father shouted angrily.

'That's right,' Charlie said approvingly. 'Would you like me to open the door so that you can be heard all over the office?'

'No one is going to hear me at all,' his father said in a more reasonable tone – Charlie had a way of puncturing him. 'And I'm not raking up any old scores. I'm only saying now what I always said. The boy was ruined.'

'He'll be ruined with a vengeance unless we do something quick,' said Charlie. 'Are you coming to Asragh with me?'

'I am not.'

'Why?'

'Because I don't want to be mixed up in it at all. That's why. I never liked anything to do with money. I saw too much of it. I'm only speaking for your good. A man done out of his money is a mad dog. You won't get any thanks for it, and anything that goes wrong, you'll get the blame.'

Nothing Charlie could say would move his father, and Charlie was shrewd enough to know that everything his father said was right. Tom wasn't to be trusted in the delicate negotiations that would be needed to get Peter out of the hole; the word here, the threat there; all the complicated machinery of family pressure. And alone he knew he was powerless. Despondently he went and told his uncle and Tom received the news with resignation, almost without understanding.

But a week later Ben came back to the office deeply disturbed. He closed the door carefully behind him and leaned across the desk to Charlie, his face drawn. For a moment he couldn't speak.

'What ails you?' Charlie asked with no great warmth.

'Your uncle passed me just now in the Main Street,' whispered his father.

Charlie wasn't greatly put out. All of his life he had been made a party to the little jabs and asides of father and uncle, and he did not realize what it meant to a man like his father, friendly and popular, this public rebuke.

'That so?' he asked without surprise. 'What did you do to him?'

'I thought you might know that,' his father said, looking at him with a troubled air from under the peak of his cap.

'Unless 'twas something you said about Peter?' suggested Charlie.

'It might, it might,' his father agreed doubtfully. 'You didn't – ah – repeat anything I said to you?'

'What a bloody fool you think I am!' Charlie said indignantly. 'And indeed I thought you had more sense. What did you say?'

'Oh, nothing. Nothing only what I said to you,' replied his father and went to the window to look out. He leaned on the sill and then tapped nervously on the frame. He was haunted by all the casual remarks he had made or might have made over a drink with an acquaintance – remarks that were no different from those he and Tom had been passing about one another all their lives. 'I shouldn't have said anything at all, of course, but I had no notion 'twould go back.'

'I'm surprised at my uncle,' said Charlie. 'Usually he cares little enough what anyone says of him.'

But even Charlie, who had moments when he almost understood his peppery little uncle, had no notion of the hopes he had raised and which his more calculating father had dashed. Tom Lucey's mind was in a rut, a rut of complacency, for the idealist too has his complacency and can be aware of it. There are moments when he would be glad to walk through any mud, but he no longer knows the way; he needs to be led; he cannot degrade himself even when he is most ready to do so. Tom was ready to beg favours from a thief. Peter had joined the Air Force under an assumed name, and this was the bitterest blow of all to him, the extinction of the name. He was something of an amateur genealogist, and had managed to convince himself, God knows how, that his family was somehow related to the Gloucestershire Lucys. This was already a sort of death.

The other death didn't take long in coming. Charlie, in the way he had, got wind of it first, and, having sent his father to break the news to Min, he went off himself to tell his uncle. It was a fine spring morning. The shop was empty but for his uncle, standing with his back to the counter studying the shelves.

'Good morning, Charliss,' he crackled over his shoulder. 'What's the best news?'

'Bad, I'm afraid, Uncle Tom,' Charlie replied, leaning across the counter to him.

'Something about Peter, I dare say?' his uncle asked casually, but Charlie noticed how, caught unawares, he had failed to say 'my son', as he had taken to doing.

'Just so.'

'Dead, I suppose?'

'Dead, Uncle Tom.'

'I was expecting something of the sort,' said his uncle. 'May the Almighty God have mercy on his soul! . . . Con!' he called at the back of the shop while he changed his coat. 'You'd better close up the shop. You'll find the crepe on the top shelf and the mourning-cards in my desk.'

'Who is it, Mr Lucey?' asked Con Quill. ''Tisn't Peter?'

''Tis, Con, 'tis, I'm sorry to say,' and Tom came out briskly with his umbrella over his arm. As they went down the street two people stopped them: the news was already round.

Charlie, who had to see about the arrangements for the funeral, left his uncle outside the house and so had no chance of averting the scene that took place inside. Not that he would have had much chance of doing so. His father had found Min in a state of collapse. Ben was the last man in the world to look after a woman, but he did manage to get her a pillow, put her legs on a chair and cover her with a rug, which was more than Charlie would have given him credit for. Min smelt of brandy. Then Ben strode up and down the darkened room with his hands in his pockets and his cap over his eyes, talking about the horrors of airplane travel. He knew he was no fit company for a woman of sensibility like Min, and he almost welcomed Tom's arrival.

'That's terrible news, Tom,' he said.

'Oh, God help us!' cried Min. 'They said he disgraced us but he didn't disgrace us long.'

'I'd sooner 'twas one of my own, Tom,' Ben said excitedly. 'As God is listening to me I would. I'd still have a couple left, but he was all ye had.'

He held out his hand to Tom. Tom looked at it, then at him, and then deliberately put his own hands behind his back.

'Aren't you going to shake hands with me, Tom?' Ben asked appealingly.

'No, Ben,' Tom said grimly. 'I am not.'

'Oh, Tom Lucey!' moaned Min with her crucified smile. 'Over your son's dead body!'

Ben looked at his brother in chagrin and dropped his hand. For a moment it looked as though he might strike him. He was a volatile, hot-tempered man.

'That wasn't what I expected from you, Tom,' he said, making a mighty effort to control himself.

'Ben,' said his brother, squaring his frail little shoulders, 'you disrespected my son while he was alive. Now that he's dead I'd thank you to leave him alone.'

'I disrespected him?' Ben exclaimed indignantly. 'I did nothing of the sort. I said things I shouldn't have said. I was upset. You know the sort I am. You were upset yourself and I dare say you said things you regret.'

' 'Tisn't alike, Ben,' Tom said in a rasping, opinionated tone. 'I said them because I loved the boy. You said them because you hated him.'

'I hated him?' Ben repeated incredulously. 'Peter? Are you out of your mind?'

'You said he changed his name because it wasn't grand enough for him,' Tom said, clutching the lapels of his coat and stepping from one foot to another. 'Why did you say such a mean, mocking, cowardly thing about the boy when he was in trouble?'

'All right, all right,' snapped Ben. 'I admit I was wrong to say it. There were a lot of things you said about my family, but I'm not throwing them back at you.'

'You said you wouldn't cross the road to help him,' said Tom. Again he primmed up the corners of his mouth and lowered his head. 'And why, Ben? I'll tell you why. Because you were jealous of him.'

'I was jealous of him?' Ben repeated. It seemed to him that he was talking to a different man, discussing a different life, as though the whole of his nature was being turned inside out.

'You were jealous of him, Ben. You were jealous because he had the upbringing and education your own sons lacked. And I'm not saying that to disparage your sons. Far from it. But you begrudged my son his advantages.'

'Never!' shouted Ben in a fury.

'And I was harsh with him,' Tom said, taking another nervous step forward while his neat waspish little voice grew harder, 'I was harsh with him and you were jealous of him, and when his hour of trouble came he had no one to turn to. Now, Ben, the least you can do is to spare us your commiserations.'

'Oh, wisha, don't mind him, Ben,' moaned Min. 'Sure, everyone knows you never begrudged my poor child anything. The man isn't in his right mind.'

'I know that, Min,' Ben said, trying hard to keep his temper. 'I know he's upset. Only for that he'd never say what he did say – or believe it.'

'We'll see, Ben, we'll see,' said Tom grimly.

3

That was how the row between the Luceys began, and it continued like that for years. Charlie married and had children of his own. He always remained friendly with his uncle and visited him regularly; sat in the stuffy front room with him and listened with frowning gravity to Tom's views, and no more than in his childhood understood what the old man was talking about. All he gathered was that none of the political parties had any principle and the country was in a bad way due to the inroads of the uneducated and ill-bred. Tom looked more and more like a rabbi. As is the way of men of character in provincial towns, he tended more and more to become a collection of mannerisms, a caricature of himself. His academic jokes on his simple customers became more elaborate; so elaborate, in fact, that in time he gave up trying to explain them and was content to be set down as merely queer. In a way it made things easier for Ben; he was able to treat the breach with Tom as another example of his brother's cantankerousness, and spoke of it with amusement and good nature.

Then he fell ill. Charlie's cares were redoubled. Ben was the world's worst patient. He was dying and didn't know it, wouldn't go to hospital, and broke the heart of his wife and daughter. He was awake at six, knocking peremptorily for his cup of tea; then waited impatiently for the paper and the post. 'What the hell is keeping Mick Duggan? That fellow spends half his time gossiping along the road. Half past nine and no post!' After that the day was a blank to him until evening when a couple of County Council chaps dropped in to keep him company and tell him what was afoot in the courthouse. There was nothing in the long low room, plastered with blue and green flowered wallpaper, but a bedside table, a press, and three or four holy pictures, and Ben's mind was not on these but on the world outside – feet passing and repassing on errands which he would never be told about. It broke his heart. He couldn't believe he was as bad as people tried to make out; sometimes it was the doctor he blamed, sometimes the chemist who wasn't careful enough of the bottles and pills he made up – Ben could remember some shocking cases. He lay in bed doing involved calculations about his pension.

Charlie came every evening to sit with him. Though his father didn't say much about Tom, Charlie knew the row was always there in the back of his mind. It left Ben bewildered, a man without bitterness. And Charlie knew he came in for some of the blame. It was the illness all over again: someone must be slipping up somewhere; the right word hadn't been dropped in the right quarter or a wrong one had been dropped instead.

Charlie, being so thick with Tom, must somehow be to blame. Ben did not understand the inevitable. One night it came out.

'You weren't at your uncle's?' Ben asked.

'I was,' Charlie said with a nod. 'I dropped in on the way up.'

'He wasn't asking about me?' Ben asked, looking at him out of the corner of his eye.

'Oh, he was,' Charlie said with a shocked air. 'Give the man his due, he always does that. That's one reason I try to drop in every day. He likes to know.'

But he knew this was not the question his father wanted answered. That question was: 'Did you say the right words? Did you make me out the feeble figure you should have made me out, or did you say the wrong thing, letting him know I was better?' These things had to be managed. In Charlie's place Ben would have managed it splendidly.

'He didn't say anything about dropping up?' Ben asked with affected lightness.

'No,' Charlie said with assumed thoughtfulness. 'I don't remember.'

'There's blackness for you!' his father said with sudden bitterness. It came as a shock to Charlie; it was the first time he had heard his father speak like that, from the heart, and he knew the end must be near.

'God knows,' Charlie said, tapping one heel nervously, 'he's a queer man. A queer bloody man!'

'Tell me, Charlie,' his father insisted, 'wouldn't you say it to him? 'Tisn't right and you know 'tisn't right.'

' 'Tisn't,' said Charlie, tearing at his hair, 'but to tell you the God's truth I'd sooner not talk to him.'

'Yes,' his father added in disappointment. 'I see it mightn't do for you.'

Charlie realized that his father was thinking of the shop, which would now come to him. He got up and stood against the fireplace, a fat, handsome, moody man.

'That has nothing to do with it,' he said. 'If he gave me cause I'd throw his bloody old shop in his face in the morning. I don't want anything from him. 'Tis just that I don't seem to

be able to talk to him. I'll send Paddy down tonight and let
him ask him.'

'Do, do,' his father said with a knowing nod. 'That's the
very thing you'll do. And tell Julie to bring me up a drop
of whiskey and a couple of glasses. You'll have a drop yourself?'

'I won't.'

'You will, you will. Julie will bring it up.'

Charlie went to his brother's house and asked him to call on
Tom and tell him how near the end was. Paddy was a gentle,
good-natured boy with something of Charlie's benevolence and
none of his guile.

'I will to be sure,' he said. 'But why don't you tell him? Sure,
he thinks the world of you.'

'I'll tell you why, Paddy,' Charlie whispered with his hand
on his brother's sleeve. 'Because if he refused me I might do
him some injury.'

'But you don't think he will?' Paddy asked in bewilderment.

'I don't think at all, Paddy,' Charlie said broodingly. 'I
know.'

He knew all right. When he called on his way home the next
afternoon his mother and sister were waiting for him, hysterical
with excitement. Paddy had met with a cold refusal. Their
hysteria was infectious. He understood now why he had caught
people glancing at him curiously in the street. It was being
argued out in every pub, what Charlie Lucey ought to do.
People couldn't mind their own bloody business. He rapped
out an oath at the two women and took the stairs three at a
time. His father was lying with his back to the window. The
whiskey was still there as Charlie had seen it the previous
evening. It tore at his heart more than the sight of his father's
despair.

'You're not feeling too good?' he said gruffly.

'I'm not, I'm not,' Ben said, lifting the sheet from his face.
'Paddy didn't bring a reply to that message?' he added ques-
tioningly.

'Do you tell me so?' Charlie replied, trying to sound
shocked.

'Paddy was always a bad man to send on a message,' his father said despondently, turning himself painfully in the bed, but still not looking at Charlie. 'Of course, he hasn't the sense. Tell me, Charlie,' he added in a feeble voice, 'weren't you there when I was talking about Peter?'

'About Peter?' Charlie exclaimed in surprise.

'You were, you were,' his father insisted, looking at the window. 'Sure, 'twas from you I heard it. You wanted to go to Asragh to look at the books, and I told you if anything went wrong you'd get the blame. Isn't that all I said?'

Charlie had to readjust his mind before he realized that his father had been going over it all again in the long hours of loneliness and pain, trying to see where he had gone wrong. It seemed to make him even more remote. Charlie didn't remember what his father had said; he doubted if his uncle remembered.

'I might have passed some joke about it,' his father said, 'but sure I was always joking him and he was always joking me. What the hell more was there in it?'

'Oh, a chance remark!' agreed Charlie.

'Now, the way I look at that,' his father said, seeking his eyes for the first time, 'someone was out to make mischief. This town is full of people like that. If you went and told him he'd believe you.'

'I will, I will,' Charlie said, sick with disgust. 'I'll see him myself today.'

He left the house, cursing his uncle for a brutal egotist. He felt the growing hysteria of the town concentrating on himself and knew that at last it had got inside him. His sisters and brothers, the people in the little shops along the street, expected him to bring his uncle to book, and failing that, to have done with him. This was the moment when people had to take their side once and for all. And he knew he was only too capable of taking sides.

Min opened the door to him, her red-rimmed eyes dirty with tears and the smell of brandy on her breath. She was near hysterics, too.

'What way is he, Charlie?' she wailed.

'Bad enough, Aunt Min,' he said as he wiped his boots and went past her. 'He won't last the night.'

At the sound of his voice his uncle had opened the sitting-room door and now he came out and drew Charlie in by the hand. Min followed. His uncle didn't release his hand, and betrayed his nervousness only by the way his frail fingers played over Charlie's hand, like a woman's.

'I'm sorry to hear it, Charliss,' he said.

'Sure, of course you are, Uncle Tom,' said Charlie, and at the first words the feeling of hysteria within him dissolved and left only a feeling of immense understanding and pity. 'You know what brought me?'

His uncle dropped his hand.

'I do, Charliss,' he said and drew himself erect. They were neither of them men to beat about the bush.

'You'll come and see the last of him,' Charlie said, not even marking the question.

'Charliss,' Tom said with that queer tightening at the corners of his mouth, 'I was never one to hedge or procrastinate. I will not come.'

He almost hissed the final words. Min broke into a loud wail.

'Talk to him, Charlie, do! I'm sick and tired of it. We can never show our faces in the town again.'

'And I need hardly say, Charliss,' his uncle continued with an air of triumph that was almost evil, 'that that doesn't trouble me.'

'I know,' Charlie said earnestly, still keeping his eyes on the withered old face with the narrow-winged, almost transparent nose. 'And you know that I never interfered between ye. Whatever disagreements ye had, I never took my father's side against you. And 'twasn't for what I might get out of you.'

In his excitement his uncle grinned, a grin that wasn't natural, and that combined in a strange way affection and arro-gance, the arrogance of the idealist who doesn't realize how easily he can be fooled.

'I never thought it, boy,' he said, raising his voice. 'Not for an instant. Nor 'twasn't in you.'

'And you know too you did this once before and you regretted it.'

'Bitterly! Bitterly!'

'And you're going to make the same mistake with your brother that you made with your son?'

'I'm not forgetting that either, Charliss,' said Tom. 'It wasn't today nor yesterday I thought of it.'

'And it isn't as if you didn't care for him,' Charlie went on remorselessly. 'It isn't as if you had no heart for him. You know he's lying up there waiting for you. He sent for you last night and you never came. He had the bottle of whiskey and the two glasses by the bed. All he wants is for you to say you forgive him ... Jesus Christ, man,' he shouted with all the violence in him roused, 'never mind what you're doing to him. Do you know what you're doing to yourself?'

'I know, Charliss,' his uncle said in a cold, excited voice. 'I know that too. And 'tisn't as you say that I have no heart for him. God knows it isn't that I don't forgive him. I forgave him long years ago for what he said about – one that was very dear to me. But I swore that day, Charliss, that never the longest day I lived would I take your father's hand in friendship, and if God was to strike me dead at this very moment for my presumption I'd say the same. You know me, Charliss,' he added, gripping the lapels of his coat. 'I never broke my word yet to God or man. I won't do it now.'

'Oh, how can you say it?' cried Min. 'Even the wild beasts have more nature.'

'Some other time I'll ask you to forgive me,' added Tom, ignoring her.

'You need never do that, Uncle Tom,' Charlie said with great simplicity and humbleness. ' 'Tis yourself you'll have to forgive.'

At the door he stopped. He had a feeling that if he turned he would see Peter standing behind him. He knew his uncle's barren pride was all he could now offer to the shadow of his son, and that it was his dead cousin who stood between them.

For a moment he felt like turning and appealing to Peter. But he was never much given to the supernatural. The real world was trouble enough for him, and he went slowly homeward, praying that he might see the blinds drawn before him.

The Long Road to Ummera

Stay for me there. I will not fail
To meet thee in that hollow vale.

Always in the evenings you saw her shuffle up the road to Miss
O.'s for her little jug of porter, a shapeless lump of an old
woman in a plaid shawl, faded to the colour of snuff, that
dragged her head down on to her bosom where she clutched its
folds in one hand; a canvas apron and a pair of men's boots
without laces. Her eyes were puffy and screwed up in tight little
buds of flesh and her rosy old face that might have been carved
out of a turnip was all crumpled with blindness. The old heart
was failing her, and several times she would have to rest, put
down the jug, lean against the wall, and lift the weight of the
shawl off her head. People passed; she stared at them humbly;
they saluted her; she turned her head and peered after them for
minutes on end. The rhythm of life had slowed down in her till
you could scarcely detect its faint and sluggish beat. Sometimes
from some queer instinct of shyness she turned to the wall,
took a snuffbox from her bosom, and shook out a pinch on the
back of her swollen hand. When she sniffed it it smeared her
nose and upper lip and spilled all over her old black blouse. She
raised the hand to her eyes and looked at it closely and reproachfully, as though astonished that it no longer served her
properly. Then she dusted herself, picked up the old jug again,
scratched herself against her clothes, and shuffled along close
by the wall, groaning aloud.

When she reached her own house, which was a little cottage
in a terrace, she took off her boots, and herself and the old
cobbler who lodged with her turned out a pot of potatoes on
the table, stripping them with their fingers and dipping them in
the little mound of salt while they took turn and turn about

with the porter jug. He was a lively and philosophic old man called Johnny Thornton.

After their supper they sat in the firelight, talking about old times in the country and long-dead neighbours, ghosts, fairies, spells, and charms. It always depressed her son, finding them together like that when he called with her monthly allowance. He was a well-to-do businessman with a little grocery shop in the South Main Street and a little house in Sunday's Well, and nothing would have pleased him better than that his mother should share all the grandeur with him, the carpets and the china and the chiming clocks. He sat moodily between them, stroking his long jaw, and wondering why they talked so much about death in the old-fashioned way, as if it was something that made no difference at all.

'Wisha, what pleasure do yet get out of old talk like that?' he asked one night.

'Like what, Pat?' his mother asked with her timid smile.

'My goodness,' he said, 'ye're always at it. Corpses and graves and people that are dead and gone.'

'Arrah, why wouldn't we?' she replied, looking down stiffly as she tried to button the open-necked blouse that revealed her old breast. 'Isn't there more of us there than here?'

'Much difference 'twill make to you when you won't know them or see them!' he exclaimed.

'Oye, why wouldn't I know them?' she cried angrily. 'Is it the Twomeys of Lackroe and the Driscolls of Ummera?'

'How sure you are we'll take you to Ummera!' he said mockingly.

'Och aye, Pat,' she asked, shaking herself against her clothes with her humble stupid wondering smile, 'and where else would you take me?'

'Isn't our own plot good enough for you?' he asked. 'Your own son and your grandchildren?'

'Musha, indeed, is it in the town you want to bury me?' She shrugged herself and blinked into the fire, her face growing sour and obstinate. 'I'll go back to Ummera, the place I came from.'

'Back to the hunger and misery we came from,' Pat said scornfully.

'Back to your father, boy.'

'Ay, to be sure, where else? But my father or grandfather never did for you what I did. Often and often I scoured the streets of Cork for a few ha'pence for you.'

'You did, amossa, you did, you did,' she admitted, looking into the fire and shaking herself. 'You were a good son to me.'

'And often I did it and the belly falling out of me with hunger,' Pat went on, full of self-pity.

' 'Tis true for you,' she mumbled, ' 'tis, 'tis, 'tis true. 'Twas often and often you had to go without it. What else could you do and the way we were left?'

'And now our grave isn't good enough for you,' he complained. There was real bitterness in his tone. He was an insignificant little man and jealous of the power the dead had over her.

She looked at him with the same abject, half-imbecile smile, the wrinkled old eyes almost shut above the Mongolian cheekbones, while with a swollen old hand, like a pot-stick, it had so little life in it, she smoothed a few locks of yellow-white hair across her temples – a trick she had when troubled.

'Musha, take me back to Ummera, Pat,' she whined. 'Take me back to my own. I'd never rest among strangers. I'd be rising and drifting.'

'Ah, foolishness, woman!' he said with an indignant look. 'That sort of thing is gone out of fashion.'

'I won't stop here for you,' she shouted hoarsely in sudden, impotent fury, and she rose and grasped the mantelpiece for support.

'You won't be asked,' he said shortly.

'I'll haunt you,' she whispered tensely, holding on to the mantelpiece and bending down over him with a horrible grin.

'And that's only more of the foolishness,' he said with a nod of contempt. 'Haunts and fairies and spells.'

She took one step towards him and stood, plastering down the two little locks of yellowing hair, the half-dead eyes twitching and blinking in the candlelight, and the swollen crumpled face with the cheeks like cracked enamel.

'Pat,' she said, 'the day we left Ummera you promised to bring me back. You were only a little gorsoon that time. The neighbours gathered round me and the last word I said to them and I going down the road was: "Neighbours, my son Pat is after giving me his word and he'll bring me back to ye when my times comes." ... That's as true as the Almighty God is over me this night. I have everything ready.' She went to the shelf under the stairs and took out two parcels. She seemed to be speaking to herself as she opened them gloatingly, bending down her head in the feeble light of the candle. 'There's the two brass candlesticks and the blessed candles alongside them. And there's my shroud aired regular on the line.'

'Ah, you're mad, woman,' he said angrily. 'Forty miles! Forty miles into the heart of the mountains!'

She suddenly shuffled towards him on her bare feet, her hand raised clawing the air, her body like her face blind with age. Her harsh croaking old voice rose to a shout.

'I brought you from it, boy, and you must bring me back. If 'twas the last shilling you had and you and your children to go to the poorhouse after, you must bring me back to Ummera. And not by the short road either! Mind what I say now! The long road! The long road to Ummera round the lake, the way I brought you from it. I lay a heavy curse on you this night if you bring me the short road over the hill. And ye must stop by the ash tree at the foot of the boreen where ye can see my little house and say a prayer for all that were ever old in it and all that played on the floor. And then – Pat! Pat Driscoll! Are you listening? Are you listening to me, I say?'

She shook him by the shoulder, peering down into his long miserable face to see how was he taking it.

'I'm listening,' he said with a shrug.

'Then' – her voice dropped to a whisper – 'you must stand up overright the neighbours and say – remember now what I'm telling you! – Neighbours, this is Abby, Batty Heige's daughter, that kept her promise to ye at the end of all.'

She said it lovingly, smiling to herself, as if it were a bit of
an old song, something she went over and over in the long
night. All West Cork was in it: the bleak road over the moors
to Ummera, the smooth grey pelts of the hills with the long
spider's-web of the fences ridging them, drawing the scarecrow fields awry, and the whitewashed cottages, poker-faced
between their little scraps of holly bushes looking this way and
that out of the wind.

'Well, I'll make a fair bargain with you,' said Pat as he rose.
Without seeming to listen she screwed up her eyes and studied
his weak melancholy face. 'This house is a great expense to me.
Do what I'm always asking you. Live with me and I'll promise
I'll take you back to Ummera.'

'Oye, I will not,' she replied sullenly, shrugging her shoulders helplessly, an old sack of a woman with all the life gone
out of her.

'All right,' said Pat. ' 'Tis your own choice. That's my last
word; take it or leave it. Live with me and Ummera for your
grave, or stop here and a plot in the Botanics.'

She watched him out the door with shoulders hunched about
her ears. Then she shrugged herself, took out her snuffbox and
took a pinch.

'Arrah, I wouldn't mind what he'd say,' said Johnny. 'A
fellow like that would change his mind tomorrow.'

'He might and he mightn't,' she said heavily, and opened the
back door to go out to the yard. It was a starry night and they
could hear the noise of the city below them in the valley. She
raised her eyes to the bright sky over the back wall and suddenly broke into a cry of loneliness and helplessness.

'Oh, oh, oh, 'tis far away from me Ummera is tonight above
any other night, and I'll die and be buried here, far from all I
ever knew and the long roads between us.'

Of course old Johnny should have known damn well what
she was up to the night she made her way down to the Cross,
creeping along beside the railings. By the blank wall opposite
the lighted pub Dan Regan, the jarvey, was standing by his
old box of a covered car with his pipe in his gob. He was the

jarvey all the old neighbours went to. Abby beckoned to him
and he followed her into the shadow of a gateway overhung
with ivy. He listened gravely to what she had to say, sniffing
and nodding, wiping his nose in his sleeve, or crossing the
pavement to hawk his nose and spit in the channel, while his
face with its drooping moustaches never relaxed its discreet
and doleful expression.

Johnny should have known what that meant and why old
Abby, who had always been so open-handed, sat before an
empty grate sooner than light a fire, and came after him on
Fridays for the rent, whether he had it or not, and even begrudged him the little drop of porter which had always been
give and take between them. He knew himself it was a change
before death and that it all went into the wallet in her bosom.
At night in her attic she counted it by the light of her candle
and when the coins dropped from her lifeless fingers he heard
her roaring like an old cow as she crawled along the naked
boards, sweeping them blindly with her palms. Then he heard
the bed creak as she tossed about in it, and the rosary being
taken from the bedhead, and the old voice rising and falling
in prayer; and sometimes when a high wind blowing up the
river roused him before dawn he could hear her muttering: a
mutter and then a yawn; the scrape of a match as she peered
at the alarm clock – the endless nights of the old – and then
the mutter of prayer again.

But Johnny in some ways was very dense, and he guessed
nothing till the night she called him and, going to the foot of
the stairs with a candle in his hand, he saw her on the land-
ing in her flour-bag shift, one hand clutching the jamb of
the door while the other clawed wildly at her few straggly
hairs.

'Johnny!' she screeched down at him, beside herself with
excitement. 'He was here.'

'Who was there?' he snarled back, still cross with sleep.

'Michael Driscoll, Pat's father.'

'Ah, you were dreaming, woman,' he said in disgust. 'Go
back to your bed in God's holy name.'

'I was not dreaming,' she cried. 'I was lying broad awake,

saying my beads, when he come in the door, beckoning me. Go down to Dan Regan's for me, Johnny.'

'I will not indeed, go down to Dan Regan's for you. Do you know what hour of night it is?'

''Tis morning.'

''Tis four o'clock! What a thing I'd do! ... Is it the way you're feeling bad?' he added with more consideration as he mounted the stairs. 'Do you want him to take you to hospital?'

'Oye, I'm going to no hospital,' she replied sullenly, turning her back on him and thumping into the room again. She opened an old chest of drawers and began fumbling in it for her best clothes, her bonnet and cloak.

'Then what the blazes do you want Dan Regan for?' he snarled in exasperation.

'What matter to you what I want him for?' she retorted with senile suspicion. 'I have a journey to go, never you mind where.'

'Ach, you old oinseach, your mind is wandering,' he cried. 'There's a divil of a wind blowing up the river. The whole house is shaking. That's what you heard. Make your mind easy now and go back to bed.'

'My mind is not wandering,' she shouted. 'Thanks be to the Almighty God I have my senses as good as you. My plans are made. I'm going back now where I came from. Back to Ummera.'

'Back to where?' Johnny asked in stupefaction.

'Back to Ummera.'

'You're madder than I thought. And do you think or imagine Dan Regan will drive you?'

'He will drive me then,' she said, shrugging herself as she held an old petticoat to the light. 'He's booked for it any hour of the day or night.'

'Then Dan Regan is madder still.'

'Leave me alone now,' she muttered stubbornly, blinking and shrugging. 'I'm going back to Ummera and that was why my old comrade came for me. All night and every night I have my beads wore out, praying the Almighty God and His Blessed Mother not to leave me die among strangers. And now I'll leave my old bones on a high hilltop in Ummera.'

Johnny was easily persuaded. It promised to be a fine day's outing and a story that would delight a pub, so he made tea for her and after that went down to Dan Regan's little cottage, and before smoke showed from any chimney on the road they were away. Johnny was hopping about the car in his excitement, leaning out, shouting through the window of the car to Dan and identifying big estates that he hadn't seen for years. When they were well outside the town, himself and Dan went in for a drink, and while they were inside the old woman dozed. Dan Regan roused her to ask if she wouldn't take a drop of something and at first she didn't know who he was and then she asked where they were and peered out at the public-house and the old dog sprawled asleep in the sunlight before the door. But when next they halted she had fallen asleep again, her mouth hanging open and her breath coming in noisy gusts. Dan's face grew gloomier. He looked hard at her and spat. Then he took a few turns about the road, lit his pipe and put on the lid.

'I don't like her looks at all, Johnny,' he said gravely. 'I done wrong. I see that now. I done wrong.'

After that, he halted every couple of miles to see how she was and Johnny, threatened with the loss of his treat, shook her and shouted at her. Each time Dan's face grew graver. He walked gloomily about the road, clearing his nose and spitting in the ditch. 'God direct me!' he said solemnly. ''Twon't be wishing to me. Her son is a powerful man. He'll break me yet. A man should never interfere between families. Blood is thicker than water. The Regans were always unlucky.'

When they reached the first town he drove straight to the police barrack and told them the story in his own peculiar way.

'Ye can tell the judge I gave ye every assistance,' he said in a reasonable brokenhearted tone. 'I was always a friend of the law. I'll keep nothing back – a pound was the price agreed. I suppose if she dies 'twill be manslaughter. I never had hand, act or part in politics. Sergeant Daly at the Cross knows me well.'

When Abby came to herself she was in a bed in the hospital.

She began to fumble for her belongings and her shrieks brought a crowd of unfortunate old women about her.

'Whisht, whisht, whisht!' they said. 'They're all in safe-keeping. You'll get them back.'

'I want them now,' she shouted, struggling to get out of bed while they held her down. 'Leave me go, ye robbers of hell! Ye night-walking rogues, leave me go. Oh, murder, murder! Ye're killing me.'

At last an old Irish-speaking priest came and comforted her. He left her quietly saying her beads, secure in the promise to see that she was buried in Ummera no matter what anyone said. As darkness fell, the beads dropped from her swollen hands and she began to mutter to herself in Irish. Sitting about the fire, the ragged old women whispered and groaned in sympathy. The Angelus rang out from a nearby church. Suddenly Abby's voice rose to a shout and she tried to lift herself on her elbow.

'Ah, Michael Driscoll, my friend, my kind comrade, you didn't forget me after all the long years. I'm a long time away from you but I'm coming at last. They tried to keep me away, to make me stop among foreigners in the town, but where would I be at all without you and all the old friends? Stay for me, my treasure! Stop and show me the way ... Neighbours,' she shouted, pointing into the shadows, 'that man there is my own husband, Michael Driscoll. Let ye see he won't leave me to find my way alone. Gather round me with yeer lanterns, neighbours, till I see who I have. I know ye all. 'Tis only the sight that's weak on me. Be easy now, my brightness, my own kind loving comrade. I'm coming. After all the long years I'm on the road to you at last ...'

It was a spring day full of wandering sunlight when they brought her the long road to Ummera, the way she had come from it forty years before. The lake was like a dazzle of midges; the shafts of the sun revolving like a great millwheel poured their cascades of milky sunlight over the hills and the little whitewashed cottages and the little black mountain-cattle among the scarecrow fields. The hearse stopped at the foot of the lane that led to the roofless cabin just as she had pictured it to herself in the long nights, and Pat, looking more melancholy than ever, turned to the waiting neighbours and said:

'Neighbours, this is Abby, Batty Heige's daughter, that kept her promise to ye at the end of all.'

Peasants

When Michael John Cronin stole the funds of the Carrickna-breena Hurling, Football and Temperance Association, commonly called the Club, everyone said: 'Devil's cure to him!' ''Tis the price of him!' 'Kind father for him!' 'What did I tell you?' and the rest of the things people say when an acquaintance has got what is coming to him.

And not only Michael John but the whole Cronin family, seed, breed, and generation, came in for it; there wasn't one of them for twenty miles round or a hundred years back but his deeds and sayings were remembered and examined by the light of this fresh scandal. Michael John's father (the heavens be his bed!) was a drunkard who beat his wife, and his father before him a land-grabber. Then there was an uncle or grand-uncle who had been a policeman and taken a hand in the bloody work at Mitchelstown long ago, and an unmarried sister of the same whose good name it would by all accounts have needed a regiment of husbands to restore. It was a grand shaking-up the Cronins got altogether, and anyone who had a grudge in for them, even if it was no more than a thirty-third cousin, had rare sport, dropping a friendly word about it and saying how sorry he was for the poor mother till he had the blood lighting in the Cronin eyes.

There was only one thing for them to do with Michael John; that was to send him to America and let the thing blow over, and that, no doubt, is what they would have done but for a certain unpleasant and extraordinary incident.

Father Crowley, the parish priest, was chairman of the committee. He was a remarkable man, even in appearance; tall, powerfully built, but very stooped, with shrewd, loveless eyes that rarely softened to anyone except two or three old people. He was a strange man, well on in years, noted for his strong

political views, which never happened to coincide with those of
any party, and as obstinate as the devil himself. Now what
should Father Crowley do but try to force the committee to
prosecute Michael John?

The committee were all religious men who up to this had
never as much as dared to question the judgements of a man of
God: yes, faith, and if the priest had been a bully, which to
give him his due he wasn't, he might have danced a jig on their
backs and they wouldn't have complained. But a man has
principles, and the like of this had never been heard of in the
parish before. What? Put the police on a boy and he in
trouble?

One by one the committee spoke up and said so. 'But he did
wrong,' said Father Crowley, thumping the table. 'He did
wrong and he should be punished.'

'Maybe so, Father,' said Con Norton, the vice-chairman,
who acted as spokesman. 'Maybe you're right, but you wouldn't
say his poor mother should be punished too and she a widow-
woman?'

'True for you!' chorused the others.

'Serve his mother right!' said the priest shortly. 'There's
none of you but knows better than I do the way that young man
was brought up. He's a rogue and his mother is a fool. Why
didn't she beat Christian principles into him when she had him
on her knee?'

'That might be, too,' Norton agreed mildly. 'I wouldn't say
but you're right, but is that any reason his Uncle Peter should
be punished?'

'Or his Uncle Dan?' asked another.

'Or his Uncle James?' asked a third.

'Or his cousins, the Dwyers, that keep the little shop in Liss-
nacarriga, as decent a living family as there is in County
Cork?' asked a fourth.

'No, Father,' said Norton, 'the argument is against
you.'

'Is it indeed?' exclaimed the priest, growing cross. 'Is it so?
What the devil has it to do with his Uncle Dan or his Uncle
James? What are ye talking about? What punishment is it to

them, will ye tell me that? Ye'll be telling me next 'tis a punishment to me and I a child of Adam like himself.'

'Wisha now, Father,' asked Norton incredulously, 'do you mean 'tis no punishment to them having one of their own blood made a public show? Is it mad you think we are? Maybe 'tis a thing you'd like done to yourself?'

'There was none of my family ever a thief,' replied Father Crowley shortly.

'Begor, we don't know whether there was or not,' snapped a little man called Daly, a hot-tempered character from the hills.

'Easy, now! Easy, Phil!' said Norton warningly.

'What do you mean by that?' asked Father Crowley, rising and grabbing his hat and stick.

'What I mean,' said Daly, blazing up, 'is that I won't sit here and listen to insinuations about my native place from any foreigner. There are as many rogues and thieves and vagabonds and liars in Cullough as ever there were in Carricknabreena — ay, begod, and more, and bigger! That's what I mean.'

'No, no, no, no,' Norton said soothingly. 'That's not what he means at all, Father. We don't want any bad blood between Cullough and Carricknabreena. What he means is that the Crowleys may be a fine substantial family in their own country, but that's fifteen long miles away, and this isn't their country, and the Cronins are neighbours of ours since the dawn of history and time, and 'twould be a very queer thing if at this hour we handed one of them over to the police ... And now, listen to me, Father,' he went on, forgetting his role of pacificator and hitting the table as hard as the rest, 'if a cow of mine got sick in the morning, 'tisn't a Cremin or a Crowley I'd be asking for help, and damn the bit of use 'twould be to me if I did. And everyone knows I'm no enemy of the Church but a respectable farmer that pays his dues and goes to his duties regularly.'

'True for you! True for you!' agreed the committee.

'I don't give a snap of my finger what you are,' retorted the priest. 'And now listen to me, Con Norton. I bear young Cronin no grudge, which is more than some of you can say, but I know my duty and I'll do it in spite of the lot of you.'

He stood at the door and looked back. They were gazing blankly at one another, not knowing what to say to such an impossible man. He shook his fist at them.

'Ye all know me,' he said. 'Ye know that all my life I'm fighting the long-tailed families. Now, with the help of God, I'll shorten the tail of one of them.'

Father Crowley's threat frightened them. They knew he was an obstinate man and had spent his time attacking what he called the 'corruption' of councils and committees, which was all very well as long as it happened outside your own parish. They dared not oppose him openly because he knew too much about all of them and, in public at least, had a lacerating tongue. The solution they favoured was a tactful one. They formed themselves into a Michael John Cronin Fund Committee and canvassed the parishioners for subscriptions to pay off what Michael John had stolen. Regretfully they decided that Father Crowley would hardly countenance a football match for the purpose.

Then with the defaulting treasurer, who wore a suitably contrite air, they marched up to the presbytery. Father Crowley was at his dinner but he told the housekeeper to show them in. He looked up in astonishment as his dining-room filled with the seven committeemen, pushing before them the cowed Michael John.

'Who the blazes are ye?' he asked, glaring at them over the lamp.

'We're the Club Committee, Father,' replied Norton.

'Oh, are ye?'

'And this is the treasurer – the ex-treasurer, I should say.'

'I won't pretend I'm glad to see him,' said Father Crowley grimly.

'He came to say he's sorry, Father,' went on Norton. 'He is sorry, and that's as true as God, and I'll tell you no lie ...' Norton made two steps forward and in a dramatic silence laid a heap of notes and silver on the table.

'What's that?' asked Father Crowley.

'The money, Father. 'Tis all paid back now and there's nothing more between us. Any little crossness there was, we'll say no more about it, in the name of God.'

The priest looked at the money and then at Norton.

'Con,' he said, 'you'd better keep the soft word for the judge. Maybe he'll think more of it than I do.'

'The judge, Father?'

'Ay, Con, the judge.'

There was a long silence. The committee stood with open mouths, unable to believe it.

'And is that what you're doing to us, Father?' asked Norton in a trembling voice. 'After all the years, and all we done for you, is it you're going to show us up before the whole country as a lot of robbers?'

'Ah, ye idiots, I'm not showing ye up.'

'You are then, Father, and you're showing up every man, woman, and child in the parish,' said Norton. 'And mark my words, 'twon't be forgotten for you.'

The following Sunday Father Crowley spoke of the matter from the altar. He spoke for a full half-hour without a trace of emotion on his grim old face, but his sermon was one long, venomous denunciation of the 'long-tailed families' who, according to him, were the ruination of the country and made a mockery of truth, justice, and charity. He was, as his congregation agreed, a shockingly obstinate old man who never knew when he was in the wrong.

After Mass he was visited in his sacristy by the committee. He gave Norton a terrible look from under his shaggy eyebrows, which made that respectable farmer flinch.

'Father,' Norton said appealingly, 'we only want one word with you. One word and then we'll go. You're a hard character, and you said some bitter things to us this morning; things we never deserved from you. But we're quiet, peaceable poor men and we don't want to cross you.'

Father Crowley made a sound like a snort.

'We came to make a bargain with you, Father,' said Norton, beginning to smile.

'A bargain?'

'We'll say no more about the whole business if you'll do one little thing – just one little thing – to oblige us.'

'The bargain!' the priest said impatiently. 'What's the bargain?'

'We'll leave the matter drop for good and all if you'll give the boy a character.'

'Yes, Father,' cried the committee in chorus. 'Give him a character! Give him a character!'

'Give him a what?' cried the priest.

'Give him a character, Father, for the love of God,' said Norton emotionally. 'If you speak up for him, the judge will leave him off and there'll be no stain on the parish.'

'Is it out of your minds you are, you halfwitted angashores?' asked Father Crowley, his face suffused with blood, his head trembling. 'Here am I all these years preaching to ye about decency and justice and truth and ye no more understand me than that wall there. Is it the way ye want me to perjure myself? Is it the way ye want me to tell a damned lie with the name of Almighty God on my lips? Answer me, is it?'

'Ah, what perjure!' Norton replied wearily. 'Sure, can't you say a few words for the boy? No one is asking you to say much. What harm will it do you to tell the judge he's an honest, good-living, upright lad, and that he took the money without meaning any harm?'

'My God!' muttered the priest, running his hands distractedly through his grey hair. 'There's no talking to ye, no talking to ye, ye lot of sheep.'

When he was gone the committeemen turned and looked at one another in bewilderment.

'That man is a terrible trial,' said one.

'He's a tyrant,' said Daly vindictively.

'He is, indeed,' sighed Norton, scratching his head. 'But in God's holy name, boys, before we do anything, we'll give him one more chance.'

That evening when he was at his tea the committeemen called again. This time they looked very spruce, businesslike, and independent. Father Crowley glared at them.

'Are ye back?' he asked bitterly. 'I was thinking ye would be.

I declare to my goodness, I'm sick of ye and yeer old committee.'

'Oh, we're not the committee, Father,' said Norton stiffly.

'Ye're not?'

'We're not.'

'All I can say is, ye look mighty like it. And, if I'm not
being impertinent, who the deuce are ye?'

'We're a deputation, Father.'

'Oh, a deputation! Fancy that, now. And a deputation from
what?'

'A deputation from the parish, Father. Now, maybe you'll
listen to us.'

'Oh, go on! I'm listening, I'm listening.'

'Well, now, 'tis like this, Father,' said Norton, dropping his
airs and graces and leaning against the table. ''Tis about that
little business this morning. Now, Father, maybe you don't
understand us and we don't understand you. There's a lot of
misunderstanding in the world today, Father. But we're quiet
simple poor men that want to do the best we can for everybody, and a few words or a few pounds wouldn't stand in our
way. Now, do you follow me?'

'I declare,' said Father Crowley, resting his elbows on the
table, 'I don't know whether I do or not.'

'Well, 'tis like this, Father. We don't want any blame on the
parish or on the Cronins, and you're the one man that can save
us. Now all we ask of you is to give the boy a character—'

'Yes, Father,' interrupted the chorus, 'give him a character!
Give him a character!'

'Give him a character, Father, and you won't be troubled by
him again. Don't say no to me now till you hear what I have to
say. We won't ask you to go next, nigh or near the court. You
have pen and ink beside you and one couple of lines is all you
need write. When 'tis over you can hand Michael John his ticket to America and tell him not to show his face in Carrickna-
breena again. There's the price of his ticket, Father,' he added,
clapping a bundle of notes on the table. 'The Cronins themselves made it up, and we have his mother's word and his own
word that he'll clear out the minute 'tis all over.'

'He can go to pot!' retorted the priest. 'What is it to me where he goes?'

'Now, Father, can't you be patient?' Norton asked reproachfully. 'Can't you let me finish what I'm saying? We know 'tis no advantage to you, and that's the very thing we came to talk about. Now, supposing – just supposing for the sake of argument – that you do what we say, there's a few of us here, and between us, we'd raise whatever little contribution to the parish fund you'd think would be reasonable to cover the expense and trouble to yourself. Now do you follow me?'

'Con Norton,' said Father Crowley, rising and holding the edge of the table, 'I follow you. This morning it was perjury, and now 'tis bribery, and the Lord knows what t'will be next. I see I've been wasting my breath ... And I see too,' he added savagely, leaning across the table towards them, 'a pedigree bull would be more use to ye than a priest.'

'What do you mean by that, Father?' asked Norton in a low voice.

'What I say.'

'And that's a saying that will be remembered for you the longest day you live,' hissed Norton, leaning towards him till they were glaring at one another over the table.

'A bull,' gasped Father Crowley. 'Not a priest.'

' 'Twill be remembered.'

'Will it? Then remember this too. I'm an old man now. I'm forty years a priest, and I'm not a priest for the money or power or glory of it, like others I know. I gave the best that was in me – maybe 'twasn't much but 'twas more than many a better man would give, and at the end of my days ...' lowering his voice to a whisper he searched them with his terrible eyes, '... at the end of my days, if I did a wrong thing, or a bad thing, or an unjust thing, there isn't a man or woman in this parish that would brave me to my face and call me a villain. And isn't that a poor story for an old man that tried to be a good priest?' His voice changed again and he raised his head defiantly. 'Now get out before I kick you out!'

And true to his word and character not one word did he say in Michael John's favour the day of the trial, no more than if

he was a black. Three months Michael John got and by all
accounts he got off light.

He was a changed man when he came out of jail, downcast
and dark in himself. Everyone was sorry for him, and people
who had never spoken to him before spoke to him then. To all
of them he said modestly: 'I'm very grateful to you, friend, for
overlooking my misfortune.' As he wouldn't go to America, the
committee made another whip-round and between what they
had collected before and what the Cronins had made up to send
him to America, he found himself with enough to open a small
shop. Then he got a job in the County Council, and an agency
for some shipping company, till at last he was able to buy a
public-house.

As for Father Crowley, till he was shifted twelve months
later, he never did a day's good in the parish. The dues went
down and the presents went down, and people with money to
spend on Masses took it fifty miles away sooner than leave it
to him. They said it broke his heart.

He has left unpleasant memories behind him. Only for him,
people say, Michael John would be in America now. Only for
him he would never have married a girl with money, or had it
to lend to poor people in the hard times, or ever sucked the
blood of Christians. For, as an old man said to me of him: 'A
robber he is and was, and a grabber like his grandfather before
him, and an enemy of the people like his uncle, the policeman;
and though some say he'll dip his hand where he dipped it
before, for myself I have no hope unless the mercy of God
would send us another Moses or Brian Boru to cast him down
and hammer him in the dust.'

Legal Aid

Delia Carty came of a very respectable family. It was going as maid to the O'Gradys of Pouladuff that ruined her. That whole family was slightly touched. The old man, a national teacher, was hardly ever at home, and the daughters weren't much better. When they weren't away visiting, they had people visiting them, and it was nothing to Delia to come in late at night and find one of them plastered round some young fellow on the sofa.

That sort of thing isn't good for any young girl. Like mistress like maid; inside six months she was smoking, and within a year she was carrying on with one Tom Flynn, a farmer's son. Her father, a respectable, hard-working man, knew nothing about it, for he would have realized that she was no match for one of the Flynns, and even if Tom's father, Ned, had known, he would never have thought it possible that any labourer's daughter could imagine herself a match for Tom.

Not, God knows, that Tom was any great catch. He was a big uncouth galoot who was certain that lovemaking, like drink, was one of the simple pleasures his father tried to deprive him of, out of spite. He used to call at the house while the O'Gradys were away, and there would be Delia in one of Eileen O'Grady's frocks and with Eileen O'Grady's lipstick and powder on, doing the lady over the tea things in the parlour. Throwing a glance over his shoulder in case anyone might spot him, Tom would heave himself onto the sofa with his boots over the end.

'Begod, I love sofas,' he would say with simple pleasure.

'Put a cushion behind you,' Delia would say.

'Oh, begod,' Tom would say, making himself comfortable, 'if ever I have a house of my own 'tis unknown what sofas and cushions I'll have. Them teachers must get great money. What the hell do they go away at all for?'

Delia loved making the tea and handing it out like a real lady, but you couldn't catch Tom out like that.

'Ah, what do I want tay for?' he would say with a doubtful glance at the cup. 'Haven't you any whiskey? Ould O'Grady must have gallons of it ... Leave it there on the table. Why the hell don't they have proper mugs with handles a man could get grip on? Is that taypot silver? Pity I'm not a teacher!'

It was only natural for Delia to show him the bedrooms and the dressing-tables with the three mirrors, the way you could see yourself from all sides, but Tom, his hands under his head, threw himself with incredulous delight on the low double bed and cried: 'Springs! Begod, 'tis like a car!'

What the springs gave rise to was entirely the O'Gradys' fault since no one but themselves would have left a house in a lonesome part to a girl of nineteen to mind. The only surprising thing was that it lasted two years without Delia showing any signs of it. It probably took Tom that time to find the right way.

But when he did he got into a terrible state. It was hardly in him to believe that a harmless poor devil like himself whom no one ever bothered his head about could achieve such un-precedented results on one girl, but when he understood it he knew only too well what the result of it would be. His father would first beat hell out of him and then throw him out and leave the farm to his nephews. There being no hope of concilia-ting his father, Tom turned his attention to God, who, though supposed to share Ned Flynn's views, about fellows and girls, had some nature in Him. Tom stopped seeing Delia, to per-suade God that he was reforming and to show that anyway it wasn't his fault. Left alone he could be a decent, good-living young fellow, but the Carty girl was a forward, deceitful hussy who had led him on instead of putting him off the way any well-bred girl would do. Between lipsticks, sofas, and tay in the par-lour, Tom put it up to God that it was a great wonder she hadn't got him into worse trouble.

Delia had to tell her mother, and Mrs Carty went to Father

Corcoran to see could he induce Tom to marry her. Father Corcoran was a tall, testy old man who, even at the age of sixty-five, couldn't make out for the life of him what young fellows saw in girls, but if he didn't know much about lovers he knew a lot about farmers.

'Wisha, Mrs Carty,' he said crankily, 'how could I get him to marry her? Wouldn't you have a bit of sense? Some little financial arrangement, maybe, so that she could leave the parish and not be a cause of scandal – I might be able to do that.'

He interviewed Ned Flynn, who by this time had got Tom's version of the story and knew financial arrangements were going to be the order of the day unless he could put a stop to them. Ned was a man of over six foot with a bald brow and a smooth unlined face as though he never had a care except his general concern for the welfare of humanity which made him look so abnormally thoughtful. Even Tom's conduct hadn't brought a wrinkle to his brow.

'I don't know, Father,' he said, stroking his bald brow with a dieaway air, 'I don't know what you could do at all.'

'Wisha, Mr Flynn,' said the priest who, when it came to the pinch, had more nature than twenty Flynns, 'wouldn't you do the handsome thing and let him marry her before it goes any further?'

'I don't see how much further it could go, Father,' said Ned.

'It could become a scandal.'

'I'm afraid 'tis that already, Father.'

'And after all,' said Father Corcoran, forcing himself to put in a good word for one of the unfortunate sex whose very existence was a mystery to him, 'is she any worse than the rest of the girls that are going? Bad is the best of them, from what I see, and Delia is a great deal better than most.'

'That's not my information at all, Father,' said Ned looking like 'The Heart Bowed Down'.

'That's a very serious statement, Mr Flynn,' said Father Corcoran, giving him a challenging look.

'It can be proved, Father,' said Ned gloomily. 'Of course I'm not denying the boy was foolish, but the cleverest can be caught.'

'You astonish me, Mr Flynn,' said Father Corcoran who was beginning to realize that he wasn't even going to get a subscription. 'Of course I can't contradict you, but 'twill cause a terrible scandal.'

'I'm as sorry for that as you are, Father,' said Ned, 'but I have my son's future to think of.'

Then, of course, the fun began. Foolish to the last, the O'Gradys wanted to keep Delia on till it was pointed out to them that Mr O'Grady would be bound to get the blame. After this, her father had to be told. Dick Carty knew exactly what became a devoted father, and he beat Delia till he had to be hauled off her by the neighbours. He was a man who loved to sit in his garden reading his paper; now he felt he owed it to himself not to be seen enjoying himself, so instead he sat over the fire and brooded. The more he brooded the angrier he became. But seeing that, with the best will in the world, he could not beat Delia every time he got angry, he turned his attention to the Flynns. Ned Flynn, that contemptible bosthoon, had slighted one of the Cartys in a parish where they had lived for hundreds of years with unblemished reputations; the Flynns, as everyone knew, being mere upstarts and outsiders without a date on their gravestones before 1850 – nobodies!

He brought Delia to see Jackie Canty, the solicitor in town. Jackie was a little jenny-ass of a man with thin lips, a pointed nose, and a pince-nez that wouldn't stop in place, and he listened with grave enjoyment to the story of Delia's misconduct. 'And what happened then, please?' he asked in his shrill singsong, looking at the floor and trying hard not to burst out into a giggle of delight. 'The devils!' he thought. 'The devils!' It was as close as Jackie was ever likely to get to the facts of life, an opportunity not to be missed.

'Anything in writing?' he sang, looking at her over the pince-nez. 'Any letters? Any documents?'

'Only a couple of notes I burned,' said Delia, who thought him a very queer man, and no wonder.

'Pity!' Jackie said with an admiring smile. 'A smart man! Oh, a very smart man!'

'Ah, 'tisn't that at all,' said Delia uncomfortably, 'only he had no occasion for writing.'

'Ah, Miss Carty,' cried Jackie in great indignation, looking at her challengingly through the specs while his voice took on a steely ring, 'a gentleman in love always finds plenty of occasion for writing. He's a smart man; your father might succeed in an action for seduction, but if 'tis defended 'twill be a dirty case.'

'Mr Canty,' said her father solemnly, 'I don't mind how dirty it is so long as I get justice.' He stood up, a powerful man of six feet, and held up his clenched fist. 'Justice is what I want,' he said dramatically. 'That's the sort I am. I keep myself to myself and mind my own business, but give me a cut, and I'll fight in a bag, tied up.'

'Don't forget that Ned Flynn has the money, Dick,' wailed Jackie.

'Mr Canty,' said Dick with a dignity verging on pathos, 'you know me?'

'I do, Dick, I do.'

'I'm living in this neighbourhood, man and boy, fifty years, and I owe nobody a ha'penny. If it took me ten years, breaking stones by the road, I'd pay it back, every penny.'

'I know, Dick, I know,' moaned Jackie. 'But there's other things as well. There's your daughter's reputation. Do you know what they'll do? They'll go into court and swear someone else was the father.'

'Tom could never say that,' Delia cried despairingly. 'The tongue would rot in his mouth.'

Jackie had no patience at all with this chit of a girl, telling him his business. He sat back with a weary air, his arm over the back of his chair.

'That statement has no foundation,' he said icily. 'There is no record of any such thing happening a witness. If there was, the inhabitants of Ireland would have considerably less to say for themselves. You would be surprised the things respectable people will say in the witness box. Rot in their mouths indeed! Ah, dear me, no. With documents, of course, it would be different, but it is only our word against theirs. Can it be proved

that you weren't knocking round with any other man at this
time, Miss Carty?'

'Indeed, I was doing nothing of the sort,' Delia said indignantly. 'I swear to God I wasn't, Mr Canty. I hardly spoke
to a fellow the whole time, only when Tom and myself might
have a row and I'd go out with Timmy Martin.'

'Timmy Martin!' Canty cried dramatically, pointing an
accusing finger at her. 'There is their man!'

'But Tom did the same with Betty Daly,' cried Delia on the
point of tears, 'and he only did it to spite me. I swear there was
nothing else in it, Mr Canty, nor he never accused me of it.'

'Mark my words,' chanted Jackie with a mournful smile,
'he'll make up for lost time now.'

In this he showed considerably more foresight than Delia
gave him credit for. After the baby was born and the action
begun, Tom and his father went to town to see their solicitor,
Peter Humphreys. Peter, who knew all he wanted to know
about the facts of life, liked the case much less than Jackie. A
cross-eyed, full-blooded man who had made his money when
law was about land, not love, he thought it a terrible comedown. Besides, he didn't think it nice to be listening to such
things.

'And so, according to you, Timmy Martin is the father?' he
asked Tom.

'Oh, I'm not swearing he is,' said Tom earnestly, giving himself a heave in his chair and crossing his legs. 'How the hell
could I? All I am saying is that I wasn't the only one, and
what's more she boasted about it. Boasted about it, begod!' he
added with a look of astonishment at such female depravity.

'Before witnesses?' asked Peter, his eyes doing a double
cross with hopelessness.

'As to that,' replied Tom with great solemnity, looking over
his shoulder for an open window he could spit through, 'I
couldn't swear.'

'But you understood her to mean Timmy Martin?'

'I'm not accusing Timmy Martin at all,' said Tom in great
alarm, seeing how the processes of law were tending to involve
him in a row with the Martins, who were a turbulent family

with ways of getting their own back unknown to any law.
'Timmy Martin is one man she used to be round with. It
might be Timmy Martin or it might be someone else, or what's
more,' he added with the look of a man who has had a sudden
revelation, 'it might be more than one.' He looked from Peter
to his father and back again to see what effect the revelation
was having, but like other revelations it didn't seem to be
going down too well. 'Begod,' he said, giving himself another
heave, 'it might be any God's number ... But, as to that,' he
added cautiously, 'I wouldn't like to swear.'

'Nor indeed, Tom,' said his solicitor with a great effort at
politeness, 'no one would advise you. You'll want a good counsel.'

'Begod, I suppose I will,' said Tom with astonished resignation before the idea that there might be people in the world bad
enough to doubt his word.

There was great excitement in the village when it became
known that the Flynns were having the Roarer Cooper as counsel. Even as a first-class variety turn Cooper could always
command attention, and everyone knew that the rights and
wrongs of the case would be relegated to their proper position
while the little matter of Eileen O'Grady's best frock received
the attention it deserved.

On the day of the hearing the court was crowded. Tom and
his father were sitting at the back with Peter Humphreys, waiting for Cooper, while Delia and her father were talking to
Jackie Canty and their own counsel, Ivers. He was a well-
built young man with a high brow, black hair, and half-closed,
red-tinged sleepy eyes. He talked in a bland drawl.

'You're not worrying, are you?' he asked Delia kindly. 'Don't
be a bit afraid ... I suppose there's no chance of them settling,
Jackie?'

'Musha, what chance would there be?' Canty asked scold-
ingly. 'Don't you know yourself what sort they are?'

'I'll have a word with Cooper myself,' said Ivers. 'Dan isn't
as bad as he looks.' He went to talk to a coarse-looking man in
wig and gown who had just come in. To say he wasn't as bad
as he looked was no great compliment. He had a face that was

almost a square, with a big jaw and blue eyes in wicked little slits that made deep dents across his cheekbones.

'What about settling this case of ours, Dan?' Ivers asked gently.

Cooper didn't even return his look; apparently he was not responsive to charm.

'Did you ever know me to settle when I could fight?' he growled.

'Not when you could fight your match,' Ivers said, without taking offence. 'You don't consider that poor girl your match?'

'We'll soon see what sort of girl she is,' replied Cooper complacently as his eyes fell on the Flynns. 'Tell me,' he whispered, 'what did she see in my client?'

'What you saw yourself when you were her age, I suppose,' said Ivers. 'You don't mean there wasn't a girl in a tobacconist's shop that you thought came down from heaven with the purpose of consoling you?'

'She had nothing in writing,' Cooper replied gravely. 'And, unlike your client, I never saw double.'

'You don't believe that yarn, do you?'

'That's one of the things I'm going to inquire into.'

'I can save you the trouble. She was too fond of him.'

'Hah!' snorted Cooper as though this were a good joke. 'And I suppose that's why she wants the cash.'

'The girl doesn't care if she never got a penny. Don't you know yourself what's behind it? A respectable father. Two respectable fathers! The trouble about marriage in this country, Dan Cooper, is that the fathers always insist on doing the coorting.'

'Hah!' grunted Cooper, rather more uncertain of himself. 'Show me this paragon of the female sex, Ivers.'

'There in the brown hat beside Canty,' said Ivers without looking round. 'Come on, you old devil, and stop trying to pretend you're Buffalo Bill. It's enough going through what she had to go through. I don't want her to go through any more.'

'And why in God's name do you come to me?' Cooper asked in sudden indignation. 'What the hell do you take me for?

A Society for Protecting Fallen Women? Why didn't the priest make him marry her?'

'When the Catholic Church can make a farmer marry a labourer's daughter the Kingdom of God will be at hand,' said Ivers. 'I'm surprised at you, Dan Cooper, not knowing better at your age.'

'And what are the neighbours doing here if she has nothing to hide?'

'Who said she had nothing to hide?' Ivers asked lightly, throwing in his hand. 'Haven't you daughters of your own? You know she played the fine lady in the O'Gradys' frocks. If 'tis any information to you she wore their jewellery as well.'

'Ivers, you're a young man of great plausibility,' said Cooper, 'but you can spare your charm on me. I have my client's interests to consider. Did she sleep with the other fellow?'

'She did not.'

'Do you believe that?'

'As I believe in my own mother.'

'The faith that moves mountains,' Cooper said despondently. 'How much are ye asking?'

'Two hundred and fifty,' replied Ivers, shaky for the first time.

'Merciful God Almighty!' moaned Cooper, turning his eyes to the ceiling. 'As if any responsible Irish court would put that price on a girl's virtue. Still, it might be as well. I'll see what I can do.'

He moved ponderously across the court and with two big arms outstretched like wings shepherded out the Flynns.

'Two hundred and fifty pounds?' gasped Ned, going white. 'Where in God's name would I get that money?'

'My dear Mr Flynn,' Cooper said with coarse amiability, 'that's only half the yearly allowance his lordship makes the young lady that obliges him, and she's not a patch on that girl in court. After a lifetime of experience I can assure you that for two years' fornication with a fine girl like that you won't pay a penny less than five hundred.'

Peter Humphreys' eyes almost grew straight with the shock of such reckless slander on a blameless judge. He didn't know what had come over the Roarer. But that wasn't the worst. When the settlement was announced and the Flynns were leaving he went up to them again.

'You can believe me when I say you did the right thing, Mr Flynn,' he said. 'I never like cases involving good-looking girls. Gentlemen of his lordship's age are terribly susceptible. But tell me, why wouldn't your son marry her now as he's about it?'

'Marry her?' echoed Ned, who hadn't yet got over the shock of having to pay two hundred and fifty pounds and costs for a little matter he could have compounded for with Father Corcoran for fifty. 'A thing like that!'

'With two hundred and fifty pounds, man?' snarled Cooper. ' 'Tisn't every day you'll pick up a daughter-in-law with that ... What do you say to the girl yourself?' he asked Tom.

'Oh, begod, the girl is all right,' said Tom.

Tom looked different. It was partly relief that he wouldn't have to perjure himself, partly astonishment at seeing his father so swiftly overthrown. His face said: 'The world is wide.'

'Ah, Mr Flynn, Mr Flynn,' whispered Cooper scornfully, 'sure you're not such a fool as to let all that good money out of the family?'

Leaving Ned gasping, he went on to where Dick Carty, aglow with pride and malice, was receiving congratulations. There were no congratulations for Delia who was standing near him. She felt a big paw on her arm and looked up to see the Roarer.

'Are you still fond of that boy?' he whispered.

'I have reason to be, haven't I?' she retorted bitterly.

'You have,' he replied with no great sympathy. 'The best. I got you that money so that you could marry him if you wanted to. Do you want to?'

Her eyes filled with tears as she thought of the poor broken china of an idol that was being offered her now.

'Once a fool, always a fool,' she said sullenly.

'You're no fool at all, girl,' he said, giving her arm an encouraging squeeze. 'You might make a man of him yet. I don't know what the law in this country is coming to. Get him away to hell out of this till I find Michael Ivers and get him to talk to your father.'

The two lawyers made the match themselves at Johnny Desmond's pub, and Johnny said it was like nothing in the world so much as a mission, with the Roarer roaring and threatening hellfire on all concerned, and Michael Ivers piping away about the joys of heaven. Johnny said it was the most instructive evening he ever had. Ivers was always recognized as a weak man so the marriage did him no great harm, but of course it was a terrible comedown for a true Roarer, and Cooper's reputation has never been the same since then.

The Man of the World

When I was a kid there were no such things as holidays for me and my likes, and I have no feeling of grievance about it because in the way of kids I simply invented them, which was much more satisfactory. One year, my summer holiday was a couple of nights I spent at the house of a friend called Jimmy Leary, who lived at the other side of the road from us. His parents sometimes went away for a couple of days to visit a sick relative in Bantry, and he was given permission to have a friend in to keep him company. I took my holiday with the greatest seriousness, insisted on the loan of Father's old travelling-bag and dragged it myself down our lane past the neighbours standing at their doors.

'Are you off somewhere, Larry?' asked one.

'Yes, Mrs Rooney,' I said with great pride. 'Off for my holidays to the Learys.'

'Wisha, aren't you very lucky?' she said with amusement.

'Lucky' seemed an absurd description of my good fortune. The Learys' house was a big one with a high flight of steps up to the front door which was always kept shut. They had a piano in the front room, a pair of binoculars on a table near the window and a toilet on the stairs that seemed to me to be the last word in elegance and immodesty. We brought the binoculars up to the bedroom with us. From the window you could see the whole road up and down, from the quarry at its foot with the tiny houses perched on top of it to the open fields at the other end, where the last gas lamp rose against the sky. Each morning I was up with the first light, leaning out of the window in my nightshirt and watching through the glasses all the mysterious figures you never saw from our lane: policemen, railwaymen and farmers on their way to market.

I admired Jimmy almost as much as I admired his house,

and for much the same reasons. He was a year older than I;
was well mannered and well dressed, and would not associate
with most of the kids on the road at all. He had a way when
any of them joined us of resting against a wall with his hands
in his trouser pockets and listening to them with a sort of well-
bred smile, a knowing smile, that seemed to me the height of
elegance. And it was not that he was a softy because he was an
excellent boxer and wrestler and could easily have held his
own with them any time, but he did not wish to. He was
superior to them. He was – there is only one word that still
describes it for me – sophisticated.

I attributed his sophistication to the piano, the binoculars
and the indoor john, and felt that if only I had the same advantages I could have been sophisticated too. I knew I wasn't
because I was always being taken in by the world of appearances. I would take a sudden violent liking to some boy, and
when I went to his house my admiration would spread to his
parents and sisters, and I would think how wonderful it must
be to have such a home; but when I told Jimmy he would
smile in that knowing way of his and say quietly, 'I believe
they had the bailiffs in a few weeks ago,' and even though I
didn't know what bailiffs were, bang would go the whole world
of appearances and I would realize that once again I had been
deceived.

It was the same with fellows and girls. Seeing some bigger
chap we knew walking out with a girl for the first time Jimmy
would say casually, 'He'd better mind himself: that one is
dynamite.' And even though I knew as little of girls who were
dynamite as I did of bailiffs, his tone would be sufficient to
indicate that I had been taken in by sweet voices and broad-
brimmed hats, gaslight and evening smells from gardens.

Forty years later I can still measure the extent of my obsession, for though my own handwriting is almost illegible, I
sometimes find myself scribbling idly on a pad in a small, stiff,
perfectly legible hand that I recognize with amusement as a
reasonably good forgery of Jimmy's. My admiration still lies
there somewhere, a fossil in my memory, but Jimmy's
knowing smile is something I have never managed to acquire.

And it all goes back to my curiosity about fellows and girls. As I say, I only imagined things about them but Jimmy knew. I was excluded from knowledge by the world of appearances that blinded and deafened me with emotion. The least thing could excite or depress me: the trees in the morning when I went to early Mass, the stained-glass windows in the church, the blue hilly streets at evening with the green flare of the gas lamps, the smells of cooking and perfume – even the smell of a cigarette packet that I had picked up from the gutter and crushed to my nose – all kept me at this side of the world of appearances while Jimmy, by right of birth or breeding was always at the other. I wanted him to tell me what it was like, but he didn't seem to be able.

Then one evening he was listening to me talk while he leant against the pillar of his gate, his pale neat hair framing his pale, good-humoured face. My excitability seemed to rouse in him a mixture of amusement and pity.

'Why don't you come over some night the family is away and I'll show you a few things?' he asked lightly.

'What'll you show me, Jimmy?' I asked eagerly.

'Noticed the new couple that's come to live next door?' he asked with a nod in the direction of the house above his own.

'No,' I admitted in disappointment. It wasn't only that I never knew anything, but I never noticed anything either. And when he described the new family that was lodging there, I realized with chagrin that I didn't even know Mrs MacCarthy who owned the house.

'Oh, they're just a newly married couple,' he said. 'They don't know that they can be seen from our house.'

'But how, Jimmy?'

'Don't look up now,' he said with a dreamy smile, while his eyes strayed over my shoulder in the direction of the lane. 'Wait till you're going away. Their end wall is only a couple of feet from ours. You can see right into the bedroom from our attic.'

'And what do they do, Jimmy?'

'Oh,' he said with a pleasant laugh, 'everything. You really should come.'

'You bet I'll come,' I said, trying to sound tougher than I felt. It wasn't that I saw anything wrong in it. It was rather that, for all my desire to become like Jimmy, I was afraid of what it might do to me.

But it wasn't enough for me to get behind the world of appearances. I had to study the appearances themselves, and for three evenings I stood under the gas lamp at the foot of our lane, across the road from the MacCarthys till I had identified the new lodgers. The husband was the first I spotted, because he came from his work at a regular hour. He was tall, with stiff jet-black hair and a big black guardsman's moustache that somehow failed to conceal the youthfulness and ingenuousness of his face, which was long and lean. Usually he came accompanied by an older man, and stood chatting for a few minutes outside his door; a black-coated, bowler-hatted figure who made large, sweeping gestures with his evening paper and sometimes doubled up in an explosion of loud laughter.

On the third evening I saw his wife, for she had obviously been waiting for him, looking from behind the parlour curtains, and when she saw him she scurried down the steps to join in the conversation. She had thrown an old jacket about her shoulders and stood there, her arms folded as though to protect herself further from the cold wind that blew down the hill from the open country, while her husband rested one hand fondly on her shoulder.

For the first time I began to feel qualms about what I proposed to do. It was one thing to do it to people you didn't know or care about, but for me even to recognize people was to adopt an emotional attitude towards them, and my attitude to this pair was already one of approval. They looked like people who might approve of me too. That night I remained awake, thinking out the terms of an anonymous letter that would put them on their guard till I had worked myself up into a fever of eloquence and indignation.

But I knew only too well that they would recognize the villain of the letter and that the villain would recognize me, so I did not write it. Instead, I gave way to fits of anger and moodiness against my parents. Yet even these were unreal because on Saturday night when Mother made a parcel of my nightshirt – I had now become sufficiently self-conscious not to take a bag – I nearly broke down. There was something about my own house that night that upset me all over again. Father, with his cap over his eyes, was sitting under the wall-lamp, reading the paper, and Mother, a shawl about her shoulders, was crouched over the fire from her little wicker-work chair, listening, and I realized that they too were part of the world of appearances I was planning to destroy, and as I said goodnight I almost felt that I was saying goodbye to them as well.

But once inside Jimmy's house I did not care so much. It always had that effect on me, of blowing me up to twice the size, as though I were expanding to greet the piano, the binoculars and the indoor toilet. I tried to pick out a tune on the piano with one hand, and Jimmy, having listened with amusement for some time, sat down and played it himself as I felt it should be played, and this too seemed to be part of his superiority.

'I suppose we'd better put in an appearance of going to bed,' he said disdainfully. 'Someone across the road might notice and tell. *They*'re in town, so I don't suppose they'll be back till late.'

We had a glass of milk in the kitchen, went upstairs, undressed and lay down though we put our overcoats beside the bed. Jimmy had a packet of sweets, but insisted on keeping them till later. 'We may need these before we're done,' he said with his knowing smile, and again I admired his orderliness and restraint. We talked in bed for a quarter of an hour; then put out the light, got up again, donned our overcoats and socks and tiptoed upstairs to the attic. Jimmy led the way with an electric torch. He was a fellow who thought of everything. Even in the attic, all was arranged for our vigil. Two trunks had been drawn up to the little window to act as seats, and there were even cushions on them. Looking out, you could at first see nothing but an expanse of blank wall topped with chimney stacks, but gradually you could make out the outline of a single window, eight or ten feet below. Jimmy sat beside me and opened his packet of sweets which he laid between us.

'Of course, we could have stayed in bed till we heard them come in,' he whispered. 'Usually you can hear them at the front door, but they might have come in quietly or we might have fallen asleep. It's always best to make sure.'

'But why don't they draw the blind?' I asked, as my heart began to beat uncomfortably.

'Because there isn't a blind,' he said with a quiet chuckle. 'Old Mrs MacCarthy never had one, and she's not going to put one in for lodgers who may be gone tomorrow. People like that never rest till they get a house of their own.'

I envied him his nonchalance as he sat back with his legs crossed, sucking a sweet just as though he were waiting in the cinema for the show to begin. I was scared by the darkness and the mystery, and by the sounds that came to us from the road with such extraordinary clarity. Besides, of course, it wasn't my house and I didn't feel at home there. At any moment I expected the front door to open and his parents to come in and catch us.

We must have been waiting for half an hour before we heard voices in the roadway, the sound of a key in the latch and then of a door opening and closing softly. Jimmy reached out and touched my arm lightly. 'This is probably our pair,' he whispered. 'We'd better not speak any more in case they might hear us.' I nodded, wishing I had never come. At that moment a faint light became visible in the great expanse of black wall, a faint, yellow stairlight that was just sufficient to silhouette the window frame beneath us. Then suddenly the whole room lit up. The man I had seen in the street stood by the doorway, his hand still on the switch. I could see it all plainly now, an ordinary small, suburban bedroom with flowery wallpaper, a coloured picture of the Sacred Heart over the double bed with the big brass knobs, a wardrobe and a dressing-table.

The man stood there till the woman came in, removing her hat in a single wide gesture and tossing it from her into a corner of the room. He still stood by the door, taking off his tie. Then he struggled with the collar, his head raised and his face set in an agonized expression. His wife kicked off her

shoes, sat on a chair by the bed and began to take off her stock-
ings. All the time she seemed to be talking because her head
was raised, looking at him, though you couldn't hear a word she
said. I glanced at Jimmy. The light from the window below
softly illumined his face as he sucked with tranquil enjoyment.

The woman rose as her husband sat on the bed with his back
to us and began to take off his shoes and socks in the same
slow, agonized way. At one point he held up his left foot and
looked at it with what might have been concern. His wife
looked at it too for a moment and then swung halfway round
as she unbuttoned her skirt. She undressed in swift, jerky
movements, twisting and turning and apparently talking all the
time. At one moment she looked into the mirror on the dressing-table and touched her cheek lightly. She crouched as she
took off her slip, and then pulled her nightdress over her head
and finished her undressing beneath it. As she removed her
underclothes she seemed to throw them anywhere at all, and I
had a strong impression that there was something haphazard
and disorderly about her. Her husband was different. Everything he removed seemed to be removed in order and then put
carefully where he could find it most readily in the morning. I
watched him take out his watch, look at it carefully, wind it and
then hang it neatly over the bed.

Then, to my surprise, she knelt by the bed, facing towards
the window, glanced up at the picture of the Sacred Heart,
made a large hasty Sign of the Cross and then covered her face
with her hands and buried her head in the bedclothes. I looked
at Jimmy in dismay but he did not seem to be embarrassed by
the sight. The husband, his folded trousers in his hand, moved
about the room slowly and carefully as though he did not wish
to disturb his wife's devotions, and when he pulled on the
trousers of his pyjamas he turned away. After that he put on
his pyjama jacket, buttoned it carefully and knelt beside her.
He, too, glanced respectfully at the picture and crossed himself slowly and reverently, but he did not bury his face and
head as she had done. He knelt upright with nothing of the
abandonment suggested by her pose, and with an expression
that combined reverence and self-respect. It was the expression

of an employee who, while admitting that he might have a few little weaknesses like the rest of the staff, prided himself on having deserved well of the management. Women, his slightly complacent air seemed to indicate, had to adopt these emotional attitudes but he spoke to God as one man to another. He finished his prayers before his wife; again he crossed himself slowly, rose and climbed into bed, glancing again at his watch as he did so.

Several minutes passed before she put her hands out before her on the bed, blessed herself in her wide, sweeping way and rose. She crossed the room in a swift movement that almost escaped me, and next moment the light went out, and it was as if the window through which we had watched the scene had disappeared with it by magic till nothing was left but a blank, black wall mounting to the chimney pots.

Jimmy rose slowly and pointed the way out to me with his flashlight. When we got downstairs we put on the bedroom light, and I saw on his face the virtuous and sophisticated air of a collector who has shown you all his treasures in the best possible light. Faced with that look, I could not bring myself to mention the woman at prayer though I felt her image would be impressed on my memory till the day I died. I could not have explained to him how at that moment everything had changed for me, how, beyond us watching the young married couple from ambush, I had felt someone else, watching us, so that at once we ceased to be the observers and became the observed. And the observed in such a humiliating position that nothing I could imagine our victims doing would have been so degrading.

I wanted to pray myself but found I couldn't. Instead, I lay in bed in the darkness, covering my eyes with my hand, and I think that even then I knew that I should never be sophisticated like Jimmy, never be able to put on a knowing smile, because always beyond the world of appearances I would see only eternity watching.

'Sometimes of course, it's better than that,' Jimmy's drowsy voice said from the darkness. 'You shouldn't judge it by tonight.'

Day Dreams

Except for occasional moments of embarrassment I never really minded being out of work. I lived at home, so I didn't need money, and though this made things harder for Mother, and Father put on a sour puss about having to feed and clothe me, I spent so much of my time out of doors that I didn't need to think about them. The uncomfortable moments came when I saw some girl I knew on a tram and could not get on it because I could not pay her fare, or when I was walking with some fellows whose conversation I enjoyed and I had to make some excuse to leave them when they went in for a drink. At times like these I was very sorry for myself and very angry with people and life.

Never for long though, and the rest of the time I was perfectly happy, for I was free to go on with my own thoughts. I wasn't opposed to work on principle because I knew a number of quite nice people who thought highly of it, but I did think that in practice people wasted too much valuable time on it for the little it gave them back. Most of the time I had worked on the railway I had been miserable, doing things I disliked and talking to chaps to whom I felt indifferent.

When the weather was really too bad I sat in the reading-room in the public library and read steadily through all the reviews and periodicals, about the crisis in British politics, penal reform, unemployment and social security. I was very strongly in favour of social security. When the weather was fair, and even when it wasn't, I walked a great deal; and because I felt I really had no right to my walks, they gave me something of the same pleasure I felt as a kid when I went on the lang from school. There is only one element common to all forms of romance – guilt; and I felt guilty about my views on the Conservative Party and social security, while all the places

I walked in had a curious poetic aura, as though each of them belonged to an entirely different country; the Glen to Scotland, the country north of our house, with its streams and fields and neat little farmhouses, to England, the river-roads to the Rhineland; so that it would not have surprised me in the least if the people I met in them all spoke different languages.

Each neighbourhood, too, had its own sort of imaginary girl; noble and tragic in the Glen, gentle and charming in the English countryside, subtle and cultivated along the river, like the big houses that stood there, sheltered behind their high stone walls. Sometimes we just met and talked since she shared my liking for the countryside; and we both realized as we told one another the story of our lives, that, different in most ways as these were, we had everything else in common. She was usually rich – English or American; and I had to persuade her about the political folly of her class, but this never seemed to offer any difficulties to her clear and sympathetic intelligence.

But at other times, perhaps when the feeling of guilt was strongest in me, she would be in some serious difficulty; being run away with by a wild horse, flying from kidnappers or just drowning. At the right moment with a coolness that was bound to appeal to any girl I stepped in; stopped the horse, scattered the gangsters or swam ashore with her from the sinking boat. Though modesty required that I should then leave without telling her my name, leaving her to a lifelong search, it nearly always happened that I accompanied her back to the Imperial Hotel and was introduced to her father who was naturally grateful and besides, had been looking for a young man just like me with a real understanding of the political situation to take over his business. If I thought of my own position at all on those walks it was only with a gentle regret that economic conditions deprived the world of the attention of a really superior mind. And the worse my situation was, the better my mind functioned.

My real difficulty came from good-natured friends who didn't, as they would have put it, want to see me wasting my time. They were always trying to get me introductions to influential people who might be able to fit me in somewhere as a warehouse clerk at thirty bob a week. I knew they meant it well, and I did my best to be grateful, but they hurt me more than Father did with his scowling and snarling, or any of the handful of enemies I had in the locality who, I knew, talked of me as a good-for-nothing or a half-idiot. 'Well, Larry,' my friends would say sagaciously, 'you're getting on, you know. 'Twon't be long now till you're twenty, and even if it was only a small job, it would be better than nothing.' And I would look at them sadly and realize that they were measuring me up against whatever miserable sort of vacancy they were capable of imagining, and seeing no disparity between us. Of course I interviewed the influential people they sent me to, and pretended a lifelong interest in double-entry book-keeping though I never had been able to understand the damned thing, and tried to look like a quiet, hard-working, religious boy who would never give any trouble. I could scarcely tell the owner of a big store that I liked being out of work. Anyway, I doubt if there was any need, because any jobs they had didn't come my way.

One night I went all the way to Blackrock, a little fishing village down the river from Cork, to see a solicitor who was supposed to have an interest in some new factory, and he talked to me for two solid hours about the commercial development of the city, and at the end of it all said he'd keep me in mind in case anything turned up. I left his house rather late and discovered to my disgust that I hadn't the price of the tram. This was one of my really bad moments. To feel guilty and have to walk is one thing; to feel as virtuous as I did after talking for hours about reclamation schemes and still have to walk is another. Besides, I had no cigarettes.

There were two ways into town; one through the suburbs, the other a little shorter, along the riverbank, and I chose this. It was a pleasant enough place by day; a river-walk called the Marina facing a beautiful road called Tivoli at the other side, and above Tivoli were the sandstone cliffs and expensive villas of Montenotte, all named with the nostalgia of an earlier day. It had an avenue of trees, a bandstand, seats for the nurse-maids and two guns captured in the Crimea over which the children climbed. It was part of the Rhineland of my day dreams, but by night the resemblance was not so clear. As it approached the city it petered out in jetties, old warehouses and badly lit streets of sailors' lodging-houses.

I had just emerged into this part when I heard a woman scream. It startled me out of my reverie, and I stood and looked about me. It was very dark. Then under a gas lamp at the corner of a warehouse I saw a man and a woman in some sort of cling. The woman was screaming her head off, and, thinking that she might have been taken ill, I ran towards them. As I did, the man broke away and walked quickly up the quay, and the woman stopped screaming and began to sob, turning her face to the wall in a curiously childish gesture of despair. As she wasn't sick, I felt awkward and merely stopped and raised my cap.

'Can I help you, miss?' I asked doubtfully.

She shook her head several times without looking at me.

'The dirty rat!' she sobbed, rubbing her face with her hand, and then she poured forth a stream of language I had never heard the like of and some of which I didn't understand at all. 'All I earned the last two nights he took from me, the rat! the rat!'

'But why did he do that?' I asked, wondering if the man could be her husband, and she gaped at me in astonishment, the tears still streaming down her little painted face. It wouldn't have been a bad face if only she'd let it alone.

'Because he says 'tis his beat,' she said. 'All the girls has to pay him. He says 'tis for protection.'

'But why don't you tell the police?' I asked.

'The police?' she echoed in the same tone. 'A hell of a lot the police care about the likes of us. Only to get more out of us, if they could.'

'But how much did he take?' I asked.

'Five quid,' she replied, and began to sob again, taking out a dirty little handkerchief to dab her eyes. 'Five blooming quid! All I earned in the past two nights! And now there won't be another ship for a week, and the old landlady will be after me for the rent.'

'All right,' I said, coming to a quick decision, 'I'll ask him about it.'

Which was exactly as far as I proposed to go. It was all still well beyond my comprehension. I quickened my step and went after the footsteps I heard retreating up the quay. Like all dreamy and timid people who will do anything to avoid a row on their own account. I have always taken an unnatural delight in those that other people thrust on me. It never even crossed my mind that I was in a dangerous locality and that I might quite well end up in the river with a knife in my back.

Some of my doubts were dispelled when the man in front of me looked back and began to run. This seemed like an admission of guilt so I ran too. Since I walked miles every day I was in excellent condition, and I knew he had small chance of getting away from me. He soon realized this as well and stopped with his back to the wall of a house and his right arm lifted. He was a tall, thin fellow with a long, pasty, cadaverous face, a moustache that looked as though it had been put in with an eyebrow pencil, and sideburns. He was good-looking too in his own coarse way.

'Excuse me,' I said, panting but still polite, 'the lady behind seems to think you have some money of hers.'

'Lady?' he snarled. 'What lady? That's no lady, you fool!'

I didn't like his tone and I strongly resented his words. I realized now what the girl behind me was but that made no difference to me. I had been brought up to treat every woman as a lady, and had no idea that a crook is as sensitive about respectability as a bank manager. It really pains him to have to deal with immoral women.

'I didn't know,' I said apologetically. 'I'm sorry. But I promised to ask you about the money.'

'Ask what you like!' he said, beginning to shout. 'The money is mine.'

'Oh, you mean she took it from you?' I said, thinking I was beginning to see the truth at last.

'Who said she took it from me?' he growled, as though I had accused him of something really bad. 'She owes it to me.'

Apparently I wasn't really seeing daylight.

'You mean you lent it to her?' I asked, but that only seemed to make him mad entirely.

'What the hell do you think I am?' he asked arrogantly. 'A money-lender? She agreed to pay me to look after her, and now she's trying to rob me.'

'But how do you look after her?' I asked – quite innocently as it happened though he didn't seem to think so.

'How do I look after her?' he repeated. 'My God, man, a woman would have no chance in a place like this without a man to look after her. Or have you any idea what it's like?'

I hadn't, and I regretted it. It struck me that perhaps I wasn't really justified in interfering; that people had their own arrangements and she might have tried some sharp practice on him. I did not realize that every crook has to have a principle to defend; otherwise, he would be compelled to have a low opinion of himself which is something that no crook likes. It was the fellow's manner I distrusted. If only he had been polite I wouldn't have dreamed of interfering.

'But in that case, surely you should let her look after herself,' I said.

'What the hell do you mean?'

'I mean, if she broke a bargain, you should just refuse to look after her any more,' I explained reasonably. 'That ought to bring her to her senses, and if it doesn't, anything that happens is her own fault.'

He looked at me incredulously as though I was an idiot, which, recollecting the whole incident is about the only way I can describe myself.

'If I were you,' I went on, 'I'd simply give her back the money and have nothing more to do with her.'

'I'll do nothing of the sort,' he said, drawing himself up. 'That money is mine. I told you that.'

'Now, look,' I said almost pleadingly, 'I don't want to have a row with you about it. It's only the state she's in.'

'You think you can make me?' he asked threateningly.

'Well, I promised the girl,' I said.

I know it sounds feeble, but feeble was what my position was, not knowing right from wrong in the matter. He glanced up the quay, and for a moment I thought he was going to make a bolt for it, but he decided against it. God knows why! I can't have looked very formidable. Then he drew himself up to his full height, the very picture of outraged rectitude, gave me a couple of pound notes, turned on his heel and began to walk away. I counted the notes and suddenly became absolutely furious.

'Come back here, you!' I said.

'What the hell is it now?' he asked as though this was the last indignity.

'I want the rest of that money,' I said.

'That's all she give me,' he snarled. 'What's this? A hold-up?'

'That's what it's going to be unless you hand over what you stole, God blast you!' I said. Now no further doubts contained the flood of indignation that was rising in me. I had given him every opportunity of explaining himself and behaving like a gentleman, and this was how he had repaid me. I knew that a man who had tried to deceive me at such a moment was only too capable of deceiving a defenceless girl, and I was determined that he should deceive her no longer. He gave me the money, a bit frightened in his manner, and I added bitingly: 'And next time you interfere with that girl, you'd better know what's going to happen you. For two pins I'd pitch you in the river, sideburns and all, you dirty, lying little brute!'

It alarms me now to write of my own imprudence, but even that did not rouse him to fighting, and he went off up the quay, muttering to himself. The girl had crept nearer us as we argued and now she rushed up to me, still weeping.

'God bless you, boy, God bless you!' she said wildly. 'I'll pray for you the longest day I live, for what you done for me.'

And then suddenly I felt very weak, and realized that I was trembling all over, trembling so that I could scarcely move. Heroism, it seemed, did not come naturally to me. All the same I managed to muster up a smile.

'You'd better let me see you home,' I said. 'I don't think you'll have any more trouble with that fellow, but just at the moment it might be better not to meet him alone.'

'Here,' she said, giving me back two of the five notes I had handed her. 'Take these. For yourself!'

'I will not, indeed,' I said, laughing. 'For what?'

'That's all you know, boy,' she said bitterly. 'That fellow have the heart scalded out of the poor unfortunate girls here. A hard life enough they have without it, the dear God knows!'

'If he talks to you again, tell him you'll put me on him,' I said. 'Delaney is my name. Larry Delaney. Tell him I'm a middleweight champion. I'm not, but he won't know.' And I laughed again, in sheer relief.

'Go on, Larry!' she said determinedly, trying to make me take the two banknotes. 'Take them!'

'I'll do nothing of the sort,' I said. 'But I'll take a fag if you have one. I'm dying for a hale.'

'God, isn't it the likes of you would be without them?' she said, fumbling in her bag. 'Here, take the packet, boy! I have tons.'

'No, thanks,' I said. 'It's just that I get a bit excited.' Which was a mild way of describing the way my hands jumped when I stood and tried to light that cigarette. She saw it too.

'What brought you down here at all?' she asked inquisitively.

'I had to walk from Blackrock,' I said.

'And where do you work? Or are you still at school?'

'I'm not working at the moment,' I said. 'That's what took me out to Blackrock, looking for a job.'

'God help us, isn't it hard?' she said. 'But you won't be long that way with God's help. You have the stuff in you, Larry, not like most of them. You're only a boy, but you stood up to that fellow that was twice your age.'

'Oh, him!' I said with a sniff. 'He's only a blow-hole.'

'Them are the dangerous ones, boy,' she said shrewdly with a queer trick she had of narrowing her eyes. 'Them are the ones you'd have to mind, or a bit of lead piping on the back of your head is what you'd be getting when you weren't looking.' Frightened by her own words, she stopped and looked behind her. 'Look, like a good boy,' she went on eagerly, 'take the old couple of quid! Go on! Ah, do, can't you! Sure, you're out of a job – don't I know damn well what 'tis like? I

suppose you had to walk from Blackrock because you hadn't
the price of the tram. Do, Larry boy! Do! Just for fags! From
me!'

She stuffed the money into the pocket of my jacket, and I
suddenly found that I wanted it. Not only for its own sake,
though it meant riches to me, but because she was that sort of
woman; warm and generous and addle-pated and because I
knew it would give her a feeling of satisfaction. Because I was
in an excited, emotional state, her emotion infected me. All the
same I put a good face on it.

'That's all right,' I said. 'I'll borrow it, and be very grateful.
But I'm going to pay it back. And I don't know your name or
where you live.'

'Ah, for God's sake!' she exclaimed with a joyous laugh.
'Forget about it! So long as I have enough to keep the old
landlady's puss off me. But if you want to see me, my name
is Molly Leahy, and I have a room here. But they all know me.
You have only to ask for me.'

We shook hands and I promised to see her soon again. Mind,
I meant that. I went over the bridges in a halo of self-satisfac-
tion. I felt I had had a great adventure, had added a whole new
area to my experience, and had learned things about life that
nobody could ever have taught me.

That mood of exaltation lasted just as long as it took me to
reach the well-lit corner by the cinema in King Street, and
then it disappeared, and I stood there in a cold wind, unable
to face the thought of returning home. I knew the reason without having to examine my conscience. It was the damned
money in my pocket. It had nothing to do with the girl, or how
she had earned it; nothing even to do with the fact that she
needed it a great deal more than I did and probably deserved
it more. It was just that I realized that the great moment of
my day dreams had come to me without my recognizing it;
that I had behaved myself as I had always hoped I would
behave, and I had then taken pay for it and in this world need
never expect more. Someone passed and looked back at me
curiously, and I realized that I had been talking to myself.

Outside the Scots Church at the foot of Summerhill an old

woman in a shawl was sitting on the low wall with her bag by her side.

'Gimme a few coppers for the night, sir, and that the Almighty God may make your bed in heaven,' she whined.

'Here you are, ma'am,' I said with a laugh, handing her the two pound notes.

Then I hurried up the hill, pursued by her clamour. Of course, the moment I had done it, I knew it was wrong; the exhibitionistic behaviour of someone who was trying to reconcile the conflict in himself by a lying dramatic gesture. Next day I would be without cigarettes again and cursing myself for a fool. I was really destitute now, without money or self-respect.

After that I could find no pleasure in my solitary walks; the imaginary girls were all gone. I took the first job I was offered, but by the time I had saved two pounds and started to look down the Marina for Molly Leahy, she had disappeared; I suppose to Liverpool or Glasgow or one of the other safety-valves by which we pious folk keep ourselves safe in our own day dreams.

The Pariah

I disliked every single one of my sister's fellows. Each of them seemed more despicable than the last. Anyone who believes in morbid psychology is welcome to make what he can of this. Maybe there was something morbid in it, but I can't help feeling that Sue brought out all that was worst in them. Because she was a girl of considerable intensity, and for short spells at least she did fling herself on young fellows in a way they weren't used to and couldn't understand. Whenever I ran into her walking out with one of them she always looked like a restaurant cat while he looked plain scared. 'Go on! Hit me!' was what her look seemed to say, but his, translated, read 'I don't really mind if she isn't safe.' She was, of course: that was the joke. It would have been hard to find a more genuinely innocent and disinterested girl, and the things they read into her conduct were only the reflection of their own timidity.

She and I quarrelled all the time about them, but nothing I ever said made her change her views about the sort of juvenile delinquent she preferred, and my mother, a vicarious romantic of an old-fashioned sort, took her part. It reached such a pitch with me that if one of them even liked something I liked, a novel or a symphony, I at once began to see weaknesses in it. My dislikes were temporary like Sue's passion, because within three months she had forgotten all about the young man, and I had forgotten completely that I had ever – God forgive me! – described Mozart as a pansy.

Then at last she started walking out with a fellow I could really respect. Terry Connolly was small, good-looking, well-educated, with fair hair and an eager manner. Though I saw that he liked me too I did not build on it, because I realized that he was the sort of chap who tries to see good in everybody. His father had died when he was young, leaving Terry

fairly well-off, but with a mother and sisters who got on his
nerves, so, with characteristic independence, he had left home
and taken a flat in town. He made no secret of the fact that he
wanted a home of his own or that he hoped Sue would marry
him. He made this plain to me the first evening we went for a
walk together, and I was deeply impressed. I liked his honesty
and his ability to make up his mind about what he wanted.

And for the first time I found myself in the position of wanting to tell one of Sue's boys that I wondered if she was really
good enough for him. It was a disturbing experience. I
wanted to be frank with Terry, but at the same time I did not
want to be disloyal to Sue. Of course, I had to concede that she
had her good points. She was warm-hearted and generous, and
intelligent so far as a girl can be who has never read anything
but what she found in the john and never has the faintest
intention of doing so. Besides, she was a first-rate cook and
dressmaker when the fancy took her, which was usually at the
last possible moment before a dinner or a dance. But at the
same time, I had to make it clear that she wasn't steady. She
took violent likes and dislikes; she was always on top of the
world or in the depths of despair, and she kept poor Mother
trailing valiantly after her, up hill and down dale. On the whole
I was probably more unfair to Sue than to Terry, but it made
no difference to him, because anything I said in her favour
only confirmed some impression he already had, while everything I said against her positively enchanted him. He thought
it delightful. He was the sort of man who prefers to see only
the good side of people he likes, a point of view I can understand, though I am of a different type myself and perhaps I
sometimes go to the other extreme.

Anyway, that made no difference either. For some reason
which I still don't understand, Sue would have nothing to do
with him, and after a few months she was insanely in love with
a commercial traveller called Nick Ryan, who was easily the
worst of all her errors of judgement. He was fat, he was
smooth, he was knowing with a sort of clerical obesity, unction
and infallibility; though mainly I remember that he admired
Proust and soured me on one of my favourite authors for a

whole year. Like Proust he had a mother, and, like Proust, he never let you hear the end of her.

This time I really let Sue know what I thought of her, and she became furious.

'You're only saying that about Nick because I wouldn't marry your pal,' she said indignantly.

'Marry him!' I said scornfully. 'As if an imbecile like you would have such luck!'

'I suppose you think he didn't ask me?' she yelped.

'Terry?' I asked incredulously. (Of course I should have known he would propose to her at once, but I still couldn't imagine that anyone would refuse him.)

'Yes. Half a dozen times.'

'And you were fool enough to turn him down?'

'What a fool I was!'

'Sure when the child doesn't love him!' Mother burst in with a pathetic defence of romantic love.

'Oh, so she doesn't love him?' I said blandly. 'She doesn't love the one decent man she's ever likely to meet, and she does love a rat like Ryan, and you talk about her likes and dislikes as if they were the law of God. You're becoming as big an idiot as she is.'

'My goodness!' Mother exclaimed indignantly. 'The way you go on! One would think you wanted to tie her up and hand her over like they did in the bad old days.'

'You're sure they were so bad?' I asked with a sneer.

'Such airs!' muttered Mother, addressing herself to the wall as she did whenever she got mad. 'That his own father wouldn't say it to me.'

'Anyway, maybe Clare Noonan will have him,' Sue added maliciously. 'He's going out with her now.'

This was a double-edged thrust because Clare was a girl I had an eye on myself, and if circumstances had permitted me to think of getting married I might even have married her. She was Sue's great friend, quiet and sweet and gay, and they made a very good couple, because Clare would do all the thoughtful things it would never cross Sue's mind to do and then look up to Sue for not doing them.

'I've no doubt she will,' I said with dignity. 'Then maybe you'll realize what a damn fool you were.'

I was wrong there, too, of course. After a few months, for all her quietness and sweetness, Clare turned Terry down flat. She said she didn't love him. I was getting very tired of that word. He in his good-natured way still continued to see her and Sue, and whenever they were in difficulties for an odd man, they summoned him in the most lordly way in the world, and he was always there to oblige, always pleasant and always generous. It puzzled me, because though I was very fond of them they were neither of them outstanding catches. They were nice girls, pretty girls, good girls, but neither was brilliant nor a beauty, and in a town like Cork where marriageable men are scarce and exacting, they stood a remarkably good chance of not marrying at all. I studied him closely, particularly in their company, but damn the thing could I see wrong with him, and I ended by deciding that what Mother called 'the bad old days' when the choice of a husband was made for them by responsible relatives, were the best days that brainless girls had ever known.

One night at the house this blew up into an open row. For some reason all Sue's friends were there, and I was the only man. Sue and Clare were whispering over the end of the sofa at one another, and I knew by their malicious air that they were talking about Terry, who was now walking out with a third girl.

'Well,' I said challengingly, bringing the whole group to attention, 'tell me what *is* wrong with Terry Connolly.'

'Tell him, Clare,' Sue said casually. 'He won't believe me.'

'Why the hell would I believe anyone who goes out with a fellow like Nick Ryan?' I asked contemptuously. This was intended to be mean, because I could see for myself that there were already feelings between Sue and Ryan. It was meaner than I intended because I didn't know until weeks after that there were also feelings between Sue and Clare on the same subject.

'Go on, Clare!' Sue said grimly. 'Why don't you tell him?'

Clare bent down and clutched her shins – a trick she had

when she was thinking hard, and looked up at me with an innocent smile.

'I don't know that I can explain it, Jack,' she said timidly. 'It's just that Terry isn't attractive somehow.'

'Really?' I said, smiling back at her, but unable even then to be cross with her, she was so sweet. 'Is that all, Clare? But don't you think we should define our terms? What do you mean by attractive?'

'Well, Jack, it's not so easy to say, is it?' she went on in the same sweet trustful tone.

'He's too blooming dull,' one of the girls called Anne Doran said in a loud voice, but I paid no particular attention to this, as Anne was the dumbest of all the decent girls that ever came out of Sunday's Well.

'Dull?' I replied sweetly. 'He's the most intelligent man in Cork but you find him dull! Don't you think there's something peculiar about that?'

'Still, Jack,' Clare said, laughing up at me, 'he is a wee bit dull, you know.'

'God's sake, woman, the man would bore you stiff,' Sue said with her brassiest air.

'Ah, no, Sue, I wouldn't go as far as that,' protested Clare in her gentle way. 'You're always taking things to the fair. I know what Jack means, and, of course, he's right. Terry is nice, and he is intelligent, whatever he talks about.'

'Sure, what does that fellow want, only a wife?' bawled Anne.

'And what do you want, Anne?' I asked. 'An establishment?'

'No, no, no, Jack,' Clare exclaimed, slapping at my feet to attract my attention. 'Anne is right too. You don't want a man just to want you as a wife.'

'You mean you want him to want you as a mistress,' I said, 'and then make him want you as his wife?'

'That's right, Jack,' said Clare, who was completely incapable of enjoying a joke and an argument at the same time and settled for the joke.

'I don't think it is right, Clare,' said a big nun-like college girl with a governessy air that delighted me. 'As I see it, you

don't like a man because you want to be his wife, but you become his wife because it's the only way you have of showing
that you like him.'

'Bunk, girl!' bawled Anne. 'As if we didn't all know it was
plain sex!'

This produced such a chorus of dissent that I left them to
it, and only realized after half an hour of it that they had left
me as wise as I was before. All I could see was that here were
half a dozen nice girls, all looking for husbands in a city where
husbands were rare, and all avoiding like the plague the one
man whom another man would have instantly chosen as the
best husband for any of them; and the only reason they could
offer seemed to be that the man was too much in earnest, made
no secret of the fact that he wanted a wife, and always looked
for the sort of girl who would make him a good one. It was
beyond me. And obviously the thing was catching, because
when Clare had shaken herself free of him, Terry knocked
round with a couple of other girls and got nowhere with them
either. The man was a sort of pariah.

Meanwhile, to my further confusion, Clare, somehow or
other, was supposed to be cutting the ground from under Sue
in her romance with Ryan. Sue was dreadfully upset by it. She
loved Ryan, but she also liked Clare and the gentle flattery of
Clare's imitation. I knew things had come to a crisis when Sue
told me that Clare was sly. Things she had said in confidence
to Clare had been repeated back to Ryan and now he would
have nothing to do with her. I found it hard to believe that
Clare could possibly be as designing as Sue made her out to be,
particularly considering the dinginess of the object, and I was
sure I was right after I had met Clare one night on the Western
Road and heard her version. According to her, she had had
nothing whatever to do with Ryan until he had come to her
and told her that everything was over between him and Sue.
She knew for a fact that he and Sue had had a terrible row
about his mother in which Sue had called his mother a designing old bitch, and that he had sworn that never, never would he
have anything more to do with a girl who spoke so disrespect-
fully of his sainted mother; and all the things that Sue was now

accusing Clare of having repeated had really been said by herself to Ryan.

'You know Sue, Jack,' Clare said to me with eyes that were full of tears.

'Oh, I know Sue, Clare,' I replied, and I saw her home and comforted her the best way I could. I had no doubt whatever that she was telling the truth.

But there was no comforting Sue, and to all my attempts at making peace she listened in stony silence, her hands on her knees like some statue of a mourning goddess.

'You don't understand women, Jack,' she said in a dead voice such as might have come from a statue. 'You never did and you never will. Clare only wants to hold on to you in case Nick might let her down the way he let me down.'

'Thanks for suggesting I might do as a stopgap,' I said. 'I'm overwhelmed.'

'I'm telling the truth, Jack,' said Sue, with the same glassy stare. 'You'll never understand how treacherous women can be. You couldn't believe a word that girl would tell you.'

So Clare in her treachery became engaged to Ryan, whom she afterwards married, and Sue took up with someone else, though it was quite clear that after her breakdown, as she would probably have described it, Sue regarded herself as emotionally dead and incapable of ever loving again. When a girl like that decides that her heart has been broken she usually makes her choice in the most arbitrary way. Why she should have chosen Ryan rather than any of the less objectionable specimens she had known I couldn't imagine, unless Clare's supposed ingratitude gave it something more of the flavour of universal tragedy.

And then one day Terry came back from Dublin, engaged. 'So he found somebody at last,' Sue said with malicious amusement. It was Sue who told me about it, and it was clear that she got a sour pleasure from all the details. Terry had been in Dublin only for a few days for some sort of conference and had met the girl one night and proposed to her the next. Even I felt this was a bit precipitate and resigned myself to the worst.

When I ran into himself and Martha in Patrick Street a few

weeks later I wondered at my own innocence. She wasn't merely nice, she was stunning; tall and thin and dark and intense, with a deep, husky voice; and it was obvious, though not in an obvious way, that she thought the sun shone out of Terry. She didn't gush; she didn't even smile or flatter; she just turned on him with a wondering air, and Terry with his good-natured manner and his pipe were both elevated into the realm of the supernatural.

She had come down to approve of the house that Terry was buying and to select the furniture for it. As he had to go back to his office, I escorted her to her hotel in King Street. For half the way we talked of nothing but furniture, and then she suddenly stopped dead and looked at me, clasping her hands.

'Jack,' she asked in a husky whisper, 'do you think I'm in my right mind?'

'I hadn't noticed anything unusual,' I replied lightly, never having seen technique like this before, if technique it was, which I doubted.

'I mean,' she said, despairingly, touching her breast with one hand and with the other pointing back up the street, 'am I mad or is that fellow as good as I think?'

'I always thought him pretty good,' I said with a smile.

'Pretty good!' she echoed at a loss for words. 'Oh, I know you don't mean it that way, of course,' she added hastily. 'I know you were always a good friend of his. But that's why I wanted to talk to you. I didn't think fellows like that existed. When I met him at a party I nearly proposed to him myself. I said it to the girl that was with me. 'I'm going to marry that man or enter a convent,' I said, and she said, 'You'll have to work damn quick because he's only here till Saturday.' And I didn't have to work at all! Do you believe in religion, Jack?' she added intensely.

'I never thought much about it,' I said, aghast at the way this extraordinary girl sprang from bough to bough.

'I don't suppose you do. Terry doesn't. He says he's an atheist or something. What the hell do I care what he is? But I prayed that night as I never prayed before in my life. I said to God: 'God, if you don't get me that fellow I don't want a fellow at all." And next night he proposed to me! On his knees! "Terry Connolly," I said, "not in your best trousers!" And you say you don't believe in religion!'

I hadn't said anything of the kind, but that didn't worry her. She clasped her hands again and seemed to rise on her toes with the ecstatic look of a saint in a stained glass window, only she was looking at me instead of at the symbol of her martyrdom.

'Honest, Jack,' she said, 'I don't know if I am on my head or my heels. When I think that after next month that fellow will be my property and I can do what I damn well please with him without anybody being able to say a word to me, I feel I'm going mad. Imagine it!' she said, with her eyes dancing. '"Stop drinking!" "Come to bed!" Imagine me talking to him like that. Sure, how the hell could I ever select furniture?'

When I left her my own head was spinning. She and Terry were coming to my house next evening, and I looked forward to it with a certain grim satisfaction. Having been crowed over, I felt I had a crow coming, and I knew it would be a substantial one. At the same time, I was surprised to find that Sue was also glad of their coming. She arranged the supper herself and spent an hour doing improbable things to a grey dress, and when the visitors arrived she answered the door herself, with her hair done up behind and a lace collar that made the grey dress into something new and strange. There was no doubt about Sue; she was always either a sloven streaking about the house with her hair hanging or else a picture. She was a picture that night. She and Martha disappeared up the stairs and left Terry and myself to the whiskey. Mother came in and Terry had a long chat with her. He was very fond of her, and she would have been fond of him if only Sue allowed her. When the girls came down again they were as thick as thieves and Sue went out of her way to be angelic to Terry. Once more, when Sue wanted to be angelic she did make you think of an angel. She even began to remind Terry tenderly of places that he and she had visited together and make him promise to take Martha there as well. Her reminiscences were

all entirely new to me, and I had never given her credit for so
much observation and such poetic feeling. For a while I had the
unpleasant impression that she was making a last-minute attempt to detach him from Martha, but that was an injustice to
Sue. She was merely giving Martha the big build-up, and in
the process was creating something for herself. Her outings
with Terry were already beginning to sound desirable. As she
was leaving, Martha gave me an embrace that almost made me
blush.

'I love your sister, Jack,' she said in a husky whisper. 'But
why the hell didn't she marry him?'

'Why didn't she?' I replied feebly enough, I knew, but with
plenty of feeling.

'I suppose it was intended,' Martha said solemnly. Intended
for her, I understood her to mean. I guessed it was.

When they had gone and Mother had gone to bed, Sue and
I sat on over the fire in the dark as we have so often done since
through the years, old cronies, really devoted to one another
yet always at cross purposes. I was waiting for my crow and
she handed it to me, handsomely, I thought.

'God, isn't she lovely?' she said with that generosity of senti-
ment that had so often maddened me when applied to young
men. 'Terry was born lucky.'

'Martha seems to think she was on the lucky side herself,'
I said, and then felt sick because I saw Sue's eyes fill with
tears.

'Don't rub it in, Jackie, there's a good boy!' she said, bending over the match I held out to her while her eyes frowned
into the cup of my palm.

'I didn't meant to rub it in,' I said contritely. 'But I was
afraid after you and Clare that he mightn't get a wife at all.'

'Poor old Clare!' Sue said in a would-be tough voice, blowing out a mouthful of smoke. 'She's the one that can really
regret it.'

'Why?' I asked in surprise. 'Have you been meeting Clare
again?'

'Ah, of an odd time,' Sue said darkly. 'She had tea with
them in town yesterday. That's how I knew about them.'

'Oh!' I said. It was gradually dawning on me that Terry's engagement had brought Sue and Clare together in one of those ways that no man can ever comprehend, as though the fact of their both having rejected him had given them a sort of corporate interest in his future.

'Ah, it's no use keeping up old quarrels,' said Sue. 'I think you were probably right about that and that it wasn't Clare's fault at all. Even if it was, the poor girl paid for it.'

'She certainly did,' I agreed. I was relieved. I knew now that Martha would have not one but half a dozen ex-sweethearts of Terry's to march in her conquering train, and for Terry's sake I was glad, because I felt he deserved it.

What I was not prepared for and do not really understand even now is Sue's belated devotion to him. But that was how it happened. For the future, when broken hearts were in fashion, Sue's would be broken for him and not for Nick Ryan, and all the places where she had been bored by him would now be touched with romance and pathos. However, seeing that women of Sue's kind must wear a broken heart for some-one, I dare say it may as well be for one of the men they have given such a very bad time to.

The Pretender

Susie and I should have known well that Denis Corby's coming 'to play with us' would mean nothing only trouble. We didn't want anyone new to play with; we had plenty, and they were all good class. But Mother was like that; giddy, open-handed and ready to listen to any tall tale. That wouldn't have been so bad if only she confined her charity to her own things, but she gave away ours as well. You couldn't turn your back in that house but she had something pinched on you, a gansey, an overcoat, or a pair of shoes, and as for the beggars that used to come to the door—! As Susie often said, we had no life.

But we were still mugs enough to swallow the yarn about the lovely lonesome little boy she'd found to play with us up on the hill. Cripes, you never in all your life got such a suck-in! Eleven o'clock one Saturday morning this fellow comes to the door, about the one age with myself only bigger, with a round red face and big green goggle-eyes. I saw at the first glance that he was no class. In fact I took him at first for a messenger boy.

'What do you want?' I asked.

'Me mudder said I was to come and play with you,' he said with a scowl, and you could see he liked it about as much as I did.

'Is your name Corby?' I asked in astonishment.

'What's that?' he asked and then he said: 'Yes.' I didn't honestly know whether he was deaf or an idiot or both.

'Mummy!' I shouted. 'Look who's here' – wondering at the same time if she could have seen him before she asked him to the house.

But she'd seen him all right, because her face lit up and she told him to come in. He took off his cap and, after taking two steps and hearing the clatter he made in the hall with his hob-nailed boots, he did the rest of it on tiptoe.

I could have cried. The fellow didn't know a single game, and when we went out playing with the Horgans and the Wrights I simply didn't know how to explain this apparition that hung on to us like some sort of poor relation.

When we sat down to dinner he put his elbows on the table and looked at us, ignoring his plate.

'Don't you like your dinner, Denis?' asked Mother – she never asked us if we liked our dinner.

'What's that?' he said, goggling at her. I was beginning to notice that he said 'What's that?' only to give himself time to think up an answer. ' 'Tis all right.'

'Oh, you ought to eat up,' said Father. 'A big hefty fellow like you!'

'What does your Mummy usually give you?' asked Mother.

'Soup,' he said.

'Would you sooner I gave you a spoon so?'

'I would.'

'What do you like for your dinner and I'll get it for you?'

'Jelly.'

Now, if that had been me, not saying 'please' or 'thank you', I'd soon have got the back of my father's hand, but it seemed as if he could say what he liked and only eat what suited him. He took only a few mouthfuls of potatoes and gravy.

After dinner we went up to our bedroom so that we could show him our toys. He seemed as frightened of them as he was of a knife and fork.

'Haven't you any toys of your own?' I asked.

'No,' he said.

'Where do you live?' asked Susie.

'The Buildings.'

'Is that a nice place?'

' 'Tis all right.' Everything was 'all right' with him.

Now, I knew the Buildings because I passed it every day on the way to school and I knew it was not all right. It was far from it. It was a low-class sort of place where the kids went barefoot and the women sat all day on the doorsteps, talking.

'Haven't you any brothers and sisters?' Susie went on.

'No. Only me mudder . . . And me Auntie Nellie,' he added after a moment.

'Who's your Auntie Nellie?'

'My auntie. She lives down the country. She comes up of an odd time.'

'And where's your daddy?' asked Susie.

'What's that?' he said, and again I could have sworn he was thinking up an answer. There was a longer pause than usual. 'I tink me daddy is dead,' he added.

'How do you mean you think he's dead?' asked Susie. 'Don't you know?'

'Me mudder said he was dead,' he said doubtfully.

'Well, your mother ought to know,' said Susie. 'But if your daddy is dead where do ye get the money?'

'From my Auntie Nellie.'

'It's because your daddy is dead that you have no toys,' Susie said in her usual God-Almighty way. ' 'Tis always better if your mummy dies first.'

'It is not better, Susie Murphy,' I said, horrified at the cold-blooded way that girl always talked about Mummy. 'God will kill you stone dead for saying that. You're only saying it because you always suck up to Daddy.'

'I do not always suck up to Daddy, Michael Murphy,' she replied coldly. 'And it's true. Everyone knows it. If Mummy died Daddy could still keep us, but if Daddy died, Mummy wouldn't have anything.'

But though I always stuck up for Mummy against Susie, I had to admit that her latest acquisition wasn't up to much.

'Ah, that woman would sicken you,' Susie said when we were in bed that night. 'Bringing in old beggars and tramps and giving them their dinner in our kitchen, the way you couldn't have a soul in to play, and then giving away our best clothes. You couldn't have a blooming thing in this house.'

Every Saturday after that Denis Corby came and tiptoed in the hall in his hobnailed boots and spooned at his dinner. As he said, the only thing he liked was jelly. He stayed on till our bed-time and listened to Mother reading us a story. He liked stories but he couldn't read himself, even comics, so Mother started teaching him and said he was very smart. A fellow who couldn't read at the age of seven, I didn't see how he could be smart. She never said I was smart.

But in other ways he was smart enough, too smart for me. Apparently a low-class boy and a complete outsider could do things I wasn't let do, like playing round the parlour, and if you asked any questions or passed any remarks, you only got into trouble. The old game of wardrobe-raiding had begun again, and I was supposed to admire the way Denis looked in my winter coat, though in secret I shed bitter tears over that coat, which was the only thing I had that went with my yellow tie. And the longer it went on, the deeper the mystery became.

One day Susie was showing off in her usual way about having been born in Dublin. She was very silly about that, because to listen to her you'd think no one had ever been born in Dublin, only herself.

'Ah, shut up!' I said. 'We all know you were born in Dublin and what about it?'

'Well, you weren't,' she said, skipping round, 'and Denis wasn't.'

'How do you know he wasn't?' I asked. 'Where were you born, Denis?'

'What's that?' he asked and gasped. Then, after a moment, he said: 'In England.'

'Where did you say?' Susie asked, scowling.

'In England.'

'How do you know?'

'Me mudder told me.'

I was delighted at the turn things had taken. You never in all your life saw anyone so put out as Susie at the idea that a common boy from the Buildings could be born in a place she wasn't born in. What made it worse was that Mummy had worked in England, and it seemed to Susie like a shocking oversight not to have had her in a place she could really brag about. She was leaping.

'When was your mummy in England?' she asked.

'She wasn't in England.'

'Then how could ye be born there, you big, silly fool?' she stormed.

'My Auntie Nelly was there,' he said sulkily.

'You couldn't be born in England just because your Auntie Nellie was there,' she said vindictively.

'Why couldn't I?' he asked, getting cross.

That stumped Susie properly. It stumped me as well. Seeing that we both thought Mother had bought us from the nurse, there didn't seem to be any good reason why an aunt couldn't have bought us as well. We argued about that for hours afterwards. Susie maintained with her usual Mrs Know-all air that if an aunt bought a baby she stopped being his aunt and became his mummy but I wasn't sure of that at all. She said she'd ask Mummy, and I warned her she'd only get her head chewed off, but she said she didn't mind.

She didn't either. That kid was madly inquisitive, and she had ways of getting information out of people that really made me ashamed. One trick of hers was to repeat whatever she'd been told with a superior air and then wait for results. That's what she did about Denis Corby.

'Mummy,' she said next day, 'do you know what that silly kid, Denis, said?'

'No, dear.'

'He said he was born in England and his mother was never in England at all,' said Susie and went off into an affected laugh.

'The dear knows ye might find something better to talk about,' Mother said in disgust. 'A lot of difference it makes to the poor child where he was born.'

'What did I tell you?' I said to her afterwards. 'I told you you'd only put Mummy in a wax. I tell you there's a mystery about that fellow and Mummy knows what it is. I wish he never came here at all.'

The Saturday following we were all given pennies and Denis and I were sent off for a walk. I thought it very cool of Mother, knowing quite well that Denis wasn't class enough for the fellows I mixed with, but it was one of those things she didn't

seem to understand and I could never explain to her. I had the
feeling that it would only make her mad.

It was a nice sunny afternoon, and we stayed at the Cross,
collecting cigarette pictures from fellows getting off the trams.
We hadn't been there long when Bastable and another fellow
came down the hill, two proper toffs – I mean they weren't
even at my school but went to the Grammar School.

'Hullo, Bastable,' I said, 'where are ye off to?' and I went a
few steps with them.

'We have a boat down the river,' he said. 'Will you come?'

I slouched along after them, between two minds. I badly
wanted to go down the river, and it was jolly decent of Bastable
to have asked me, but I was tied to Denis, who wasn't class
enough to bring with me even if he was asked.

'I'm with this fellow,' I said with a sigh, and Bastable looked
back at Denis, who was sitting on the high wall over the church,
and realized at the first glance that he wouldn't do.

'Ah, boy, you don't know what you're missing,' he said.

I knew that only too well. I looked up and there was Denis,
goggling down at us, close enough to remind me of the miserable sort of afternoon I'd have to spend with him if I stayed,
but far enough away not to be on my conscience too much.

'Denis,' I shouted, 'I'm going down a bit of the way with
these chaps. You can wait for me if you like.'

Then I began to run and the others ran with me. I felt rather
ashamed, but at the time I really did intend not to stay long
with them. Of course, once I got to the river I forgot all my
good resolutions – you know the way it is with boats – and it
wasn't until I was coming back up the avenue in the dusk and
noticed the gas lamps lit that I realized how late it was and
my heart sank. I was really soft-hearted and I felt full of pity
for poor old Denis waiting there for me all the time. When I
reached the Cross and found he wasn't there it only made it
worse, because it must have meant he'd given me up and gone
home. I was very upset about it particularly about what I was
going to say to the mother.

When I reached home I found the front door open and the
kitchen in darkness. I went in quietly and to my astonishment I

saw Mother and Denis sitting together over the fire. I just can't describe the extraordinary impression they made on me. They looked so snug, sitting there together in the firelight, that they made me feel like an outsider. I came in conscience-stricken and intending to bluff, and instead I suddenly found myself wanting to cry, I didn't know for what reason.

'Hullo,' Denis said, giving me a grin, 'where did you go?'

'Ah, just down the river with Bastable,' I said, hanging up my cap and trying to sound casual. 'Where did you get to?'

'I came back,' he said still grinning.

'And indeed, Michael, you should be thoroughly ashamed of yourself, leaving Denis like that,' Mother said sharply.

'But really, Mummy, I didn't,' I said weakly. 'I only just went down a bit of the way with them, that's all.'

I found it difficult enough to get even that much out without blubbing. Denis Corby had turned the tables on me with a vengeance. It was I who was jealous, and it took me weeks to see why. Then I suddenly tumbled to the fact that though he was quite ready to play with Susie and me it wasn't for that he came to the house. It was Mother, not us, he was interested in. He even arranged things so that he didn't have to come with us and could stay behind with her. Even when she didn't want him in the house he was content to sit on the wall outside just to have her to himself if she came to the door or wanted someone to run a message for her. It was only then that my suspicions turned to panic. After that I was afraid of leaving him behind me because of what he might do or say when my back was turned. And of course he knew I knew what was in his mind, and dared me.

One day I had to go on a message to the Cross and I asked him to come. He wouldn't; he said he wanted to stay and play with Susie, and she, flattered at what she thought were his attentions, took his part.

'Go on now, Michael Murphy!' she said in her bossy way. 'You were sent on the message and you can go by yourself. Denis is stopping here with me.'

'It's not you he wants to stop with, you little fool!' I said, losing my patience with her. 'It's Mummy.'

'It is not,' he said, and I saw from the way he reddened that he knew I had him caught.

'It is,' I said truculently. 'You're always doing it. You'd better let her alone. She's not your mother.'

'She's my aunt,' he said sullenly.

'That's a lie,' I shouted, beside myself with rage. 'She's not your aunt.'

'She told me to call her that,' he said.

'That has nothing to do with it,' I said. 'She's my mummy, not yours.'

He suddenly gave me a queer look.

'How do you know?' he asked in a low voice.

For a moment I was too stunned to speak. It had never struck me before that if his Aunt Nellie could be his mother, Mummy, whom he called Aunt Kate, could be his mother as well. In fact, anyone could be a fellow's mother if only he knew. My only chance was to brazen it out.

'She couldn't be,' I said. 'Your mother lives up the Buildings.'

'She's not me mudder,' he said in the same low voice.

'Oh, there's a thing to say!' I cried, though the stupefaction was put on.

'How could she be me mudder?' he went on. 'She was never in England.'

The mystery was so close I felt I could solve it in a few words if only I knew which. Of course it was possible that Mother, having worked in England, could be his real mother while his own mother couldn't, and this was what had been between them both from the start. The shock of it was almost more than I could bear. I could keep my end up at all only by pretending to be scandalized.

'Oh,' I cried, 'I'll tell her what you said.'

'You can if you like,' he replied sullenly.

And of course he knew I couldn't. Whatever strange hold he had over her, you simply daren't ask her a reasonable question about him.

Susie was watching the pair of us curiously. She felt there

was something wrong but didn't know what. I tried to en-
lighten her that night in bed: how it all fitted in, his mother
who couldn't be his mother because she'd never been to England, his Aunt Nellie who could but probably wasn't because
he saw so little of her, and Mummy who had not only been to
England but saw him every week, made a pet of him, and
wouldn't let you say a word against him. Susie agreed that this
was quite probable, but she was as heartless as usual about
it.

'She can be his mummy if she likes,' she said with a shrug.
'I don't care.'

'That's only because you're Daddy's pet,' I said.

'It is not, Michael Murphy, but it doesn't make any difference what she is so long as he only comes every Saturday.'

'You wait,' I whispered threateningly. 'You'll see if his
mother dies he'll come and live here. Then you'll be sorry.'

Susie couldn't see the seriousness of it because she was never
Mummy's pet as I was, and didn't see how Denis Corby was
gradually replacing us both in Mother's affection, or how day
after day she mentioned him only to praise him or compare him
with us. I got heart-scalded hearing how good he was. I
couldn't be good in that sly, insinuating way, just trying to get
inside other people. I tried, but it was no use, and after a while
I lost heart and never seemed to be out of mischief. I didn't
know what was wrong with me, but I was always breaking,
losing, pinching. Mother didn't know either and only got more
impatient with me.

'I don't know under God what's come over you,' she said
angrily. 'Every week that passes you're becoming more and
more of a savage.'

As if I could be anything else, knowing what I knew! It was
Denis, Denis, Denis the whole time. Denis was sick and had to
be taken to a doctor and the doctor said he was worrying about
something. Nothing was said about the way I was worrying,
seeing him turn me into a stranger in my own house. By this
time I was really desperate.

It came to a head one day when Mother asked me to go on a
message. I broke down and said I didn't want to. Mother in her

fury couldn't see that it was only because I'd be leaving Denis behind me.

'All right, all right,' she snapped. 'I'll send Denis. I'm fed up with you.'

But this was worse. This was the end of everything, the final proof that I had been replaced.

'No, no, Mummy, I'll go, I'll go,' I said, and I took the money and went out sobbing. Denis Corby was sitting on the wall and Susie and two other little girls were playing pickie on the garden path. Susie looked at me in surprise, her left leg still lifted.

'What ails you?' she asked.

'I have to go on a message,' I said, bawling like a kid.

'Well, that's nothing to cry about.'

'I have to go by myself,' I wailed, though I knew well it was a silly complaint, a baby's complaint, and one I'd never have made in my right mind. Susie saw that too, and she was torn between the desire to go on with her game and to come with me to find out what was wrong.

'Can't Denis go with you?' she asked, tossing the hair from her eyes.

'He wouldn't come,' I sobbed.

'You never asked me,' he said in a loud, surly voice.

'Go on!' I said, blind with misery and rage. 'You never come anywhere with me. You're only wanting to go in to my mother.'

'I am not,' he shouted.

'You are, Denis Corby,' Susie said suddenly in a shrill, scolding voice, and I realized that she had at last seen the truth for herself and come down on my side. 'You're always doing it. You don't come here to play with us at all.'

'I do.'

'You don't, you don't,' I hissed, losing all control of myself and going up to him with my fists clenched. 'You Indian witch!'

It was the most deadly insult I could think of, and it roused him. He got off the wall and faced Susie and me, his hands hanging, his face like a lantern.

'I'm not an Indian witch,' he said with smouldering anger.

'You are an Indian witch, you are an Indian witch,' I said and gave him the coward's blow, straight in the face. He didn't try to hit back though he was twice my size, a proper little sissy.

'God help us!' one of the little girls bawled. 'You ought to be ashamed of yourself, hitting the little boy like that, Michael Murphy.'

'Then he ought to let our mummy alone,' Susie screeched. Now that she saw the others turn against me she was dancing with rage, a real little virago. 'He's always trying to make out that she's his mummy, and she isn't.'

'I never said she was my mummy,' he said, sulky and frightened.

'You did say it,' I said, and I hit him again, in the chest this time. 'You're trying to make out that I'm your brother and I'm not.'

'And I'm not your sister either,' Susie screeched defiantly, doing a war-dance about him. 'I'm Michael Murphy's sister, and I'm not your sister, and if you say I am again I'll tell my daddy on you.'

'Michael, Michael Murphy! Susie! What are you doing to the little boy?' shouted a wrathful voice, and when I looked up there was an officious neighbour, clapping her hands from the gate at us. There were others out as well. We had been all shouting so loudly that we had gathered an audience. Suddenly Susie and I got two clouts that sent us flying.

'What in God's holy name is the meaning of this?' cried Mother, taking Denis by the hand. 'How dare you strike that child, you dirty little corner-boy?'

Then she turned and swept in with Denis, leaving the rest of us flabbergasted.

'Now we'll all be killed,' Susie snivelled, between pain and fright. 'She'll murder us. And 'twas all your fault, Michael Murphy.'

But by then I didn't care what happened. Denis Corby had won at last and even before the neighbours was treated as Mother's pet. In an excited tone Susie began telling the other girls about Denis and all his different mothers and all the troubles they had brought on us.

He was inside a long time, a very long time it seemed to me. Then he came out by himself and it was only afterwards I remembered that he did it on tiptoe. Mother looked like murder all that day. The following Saturday Denis didn't come at all and the Saturday after Mother sent Susie and me up to the Buildings for him.

By that time I didn't really mind and I bore him no grudge for what had happened. Mother had explained to us that she wasn't really his mother, and that, in fact, he hadn't any proper mother. This was what she had told him when she brought him in, and it seems it was a nasty shock to him. You could understand that, of course. If a fellow really did think someone was his mother and then found she wasn't it would be quite a shock. I was full of compassion for him really. The whole week I'd been angelic – even Mummy admitted that.

When we went in he was sitting at the fire with his mother – the one he thought at first was his mother. She made a fuss of Susie and me and said what lovely children we were. I didn't like her very much myself. I thought her too sweet to be wholesome.

'Go on back with them now, Dinny boy,' she said, pawing him on the knee. 'Sure you haven't a soul to play with in this old hole.'

But he wouldn't come, and nothing we said could make him. He treated us like enemies, almost. Really I suppose he felt a bit of a fool. His mother was a wrinkled old woman; the house was only a labourer's cottage without even an upstairs room; you could see they were no class, and as I said to Susie on the way home, the fellow had a cool cheek to imagine we were his brother and sister.

Expectation of Life

When Shiela Hennessey married Jim Gaffney, a man twenty years older than herself, we were all pleased and rather surprised. By that time we were sure she wouldn't marry at all. Her father had been a small builder, and one of the town jokers put it down to a hereditary distaste of contracts.

Besides, she had been keeping company with Matt Sheridan off and on for ten years. Matt, who was a quiet chap, let on to be interested only in the bit of money her father had left her, but he was really very much in love with her, and, to give her her due, she had been as much in love with him as time and other young men permitted. Shiela had to a pronounced extent the feminine weakness for second strings. Suddenly she would scare off the prospect of a long life with a pleasant, quiet man like Matt, and for six months or so would run a tearing line with some young fellow from the College. At first Matt resented this, but later he either grew resigned or developed the only technique for handling it because he turned it all into a great joke, and called her young man of the moment 'the spare wheel'.

And she really did get something out of those romances. A fellow called Magennis left her with a sound appreciation of Jane Austen and Bach, while another, Jack Mortimer, who was unhappy at home, taught her to admire Henry James and persuaded her that she had a father fixation. But all of them were pretty unsuitable, and Matt in his quiet, determined way knew that if only he could sit tight and give no sign of jealousy and encourage her to analyse their characters, she would eventually be bound to analyse herself out of love altogether. Until the next time, of course, but he had the hope that one of these days she would tire of her experiments and turn to him for good. At the same time, like the rest of us he realized that she might not marry at all. She was just the type of pious, well-courted, dissatisfied girl who as often as not ends up in a convent, but he was in no hurry and prepared to take a chance.

And no doubt, unless she had done this, she would have married him eventually only that she fell violently in love with Jim Gaffney. Jim was a man in his early fifties, small and stout and good-natured. He was a widower with a grown son in Dublin, a little business on the Grand Parade and a queer old house on Fair Hill, and as if these weren't drawbacks enough for anyone, he was a man with no religious beliefs worth mentioning.

According to Shiela's own story which was as liable as not to be true, it was she who had to do all the courting and she who had to propose. It seemed that Jim had the Gaffney expectation of life worked out over three generations, and according to this he had only eight years to go, so that even when she did propose he practically refused her.

'And what are you going to do with yourself when the eight years are up?' asked Matt when she broke the news to him.

'I haven't even thought about it, Matt,' she said. 'All I know is that eight years with Jim would be more to me than a lifetime with anyone else.'

'Oh, well,' he said with a bitter little smile, 'I suppose you and I had better say goodbye.'

'But you will stay friends with me, Matt?' she asked anxiously.

'I will not, Shiela,' he replied with sudden violence. 'The less I see of you from this onwards, the better pleased I'll be.'

'You're not really as bitter as that with me,' she said in distress.

'I don't know whether I am or not,' he said flatly. 'I just don't want to be mixed up with you after this. To tell you the truth, I don't believe you give a damn for this fellow.'

'But I do, Matt. Why do you think I'm marrying him?'

'I think you're marrying him because you're hopelessly spoiled and neurotic, and ready for any silly adventure. What does your mother say to it?'

'Mummy will get used to Jim in time.'

'Excuse my saying so, Shiela, but your mother will do nothing of the sort. If your father was alive he'd beat the hell out of you before he let you do it. Is it someone of his own age? Talk sense! By the time you're forty he'll be a doddering old man. How can it end in anything but trouble?'

'Matt, I don't care what it ends in. That's my lookout. All I want is for you and Jim to be friends.'

It wasn't so much that Shiela wanted them to be friends as that she wanted to preserve her claim on Matt. Women are like that. They hate to let one man go even when they have sworn lifelong fidelity to another.

'I have no desire to be friends,' said Matt angrily. 'I've wasted enough of my life on you as it is.'

'I wish you wouldn't say things like that, Matt,' she said, beginning to sniff. 'I know I'm queer. I suppose I'm not normal. Jack Mortimer always said I had a father fixation, but what can I do about that? I know you think I just strung you along all these years but you're wrong about that. I cared more for you than I did for all the others and you know it. And if it wasn't for Jim I'd marry you now sooner than anybody.'

'Oh, if it wasn't for Jim,' he said mockingly. 'If it wasn't Jim it would be somebody else, and I'm tired of it. It's all very well being patient, Shiela, but a man reaches the point where he has to protect himself, even if it hurts him or someone else. I've reached it.'

And she knew he had, and that she had no hope of holding on to him. A man who had stuck to her for all those years and through all her vagaries was not the sort to be summoned back by a whim. Parting with him was more of a wrench than she had anticipated.

2

She was radiantly happy through their brief honeymoon in France. She had always been fascinated and repelled by sex, and on their first night on the boat, Jim, instead of making violent love to her as a younger man might have done, sat on his bunk and made her listen to a long lecture on the subject which she found more interesting than any lovemaking; and before they had been married a week, she was making the difficult adjustment for herself and without shock.

As a companion Jim was excellent because he was ready to be pleased with everything from urinals to cathedrals; he got as much pleasure out of small things as big ones, and it put her in good humour just to see the way he enjoyed himself. He would sit in the sunlight outside a café, a bulky man with a red face and white hair, enthusing over his pastries and coffee and the spectacle of good-looking, well-dressed people going by. When his face clouded it was only because he had remembered the folly of those who would not be happy when they could.

'And the whoors at home won't even learn how to make a cup of coffee!' he would declare bitterly.

The only times he got mad were when Shiela, tall and tangential, moved too fast for him, and he had to shuffle after her on his tender feet, swinging his arms close to his chest like a runner, or when she suddenly changed her mind at a crossing and left him in the middle of the traffic to run forward and back, alarmed and swearing. In his rage he shouted and shook his fist at the taxi-drivers and they shouted back at him without his even knowing what they said. At times like these he even shouted at Shiela, and she promised in the future to wait for him but she didn't. She was a born fidget, and when he left her somewhere to go to one of his beloved urinals she drifted on to the nearest shop window and he lost her. Because all the French he knew came from the North Monastery and French policemen only looked astonished when they heard it, and because he could never remember the name of his hotel, he was plunged in despair once a day.

It was a great relief to him to get back to Fair Hill, put his feet on the mantelpiece and study in books the places he had been. Shiela too came to understand how good a marriage could be, with the inhibitions of a lifetime breaking down and new and more complicated ones taking their place. Their life was exceedingly quiet. Each evening Jim came puffing up the hill from town under a mountain of pullovers, scarves and coats, saying that the damn height was getting too much for him, and that they'd have to – have to – have to, get a house in town. Then he changed into old trousers and slippers and lovingly poured himself a glass of whiskey, the whiskey carefully measured against the light as it had been any time in twenty years. He knew to a drop the amount of spirits it needed to give him the feeling of a proper drink without slugging himself. Only a man with a steady hand could know how much was good for him. Moderation was the secret.

After supper he put his feet on the mantelpiece and told her the day's news from town. About nine they had a cup of tea, and if the night was fine took a short ramble over the hill to get the view of the illuminated city below. By this time, as Shiela had learned, Jim was at the top of his form and it had become unsafe for anyone to suggest a house in town. Fair Hill had again become the perfect place of residence. The tension of the day completely gone, he had his bath and pottered about the stiff, ungainly old house in his pyjama trousers, scratching himself in elaborate patterns and roaring with laughter at his own jokes.

'Who the hell said I had a father fixation?' Shiela asked indignantly. 'I didn't marry my father; I married my baby.'

All the same, she knew he wasn't all that simple. Paddy, his son, lived in Dublin, and though Shiela suspected that he was somewhat of a disappointment to Jim, she could never get a really coherent account of him from Jim. It was the same with his first marriage. He scarcely spoke of it except once in a while to say 'Margaret used to think' or 'a friend of Margaret's' – bubbles rising to the surface of a pool whose depths she could not see though she suspected the shadow that covered it. Nor was he much more informative about less intimate matters. If he disliked people, he disliked talking of them, and if he liked them, he only wished to say conventional things in their praise. As a student of Jane Austen and Henry James, Shiela wanted to plumb things to their depths, and sometimes it made her very angry that he would not argue with her. It suggested that he did not take her seriously.

'What is it about Kitty O'Malley that makes her get in

with all those extraordinary men?' she would ask. 'Is it a reaction against her mother?'

'Begor, I don't know, girl,' he would say, staring at her over his reading glasses as though he were a simpleminded man to whom such difficult problems never occurred.

'And I suppose you never bothered to ask yourself,' she would retort angrily. 'You prefer to know people superficially.'

'Ah, well, I'm a superficial sort of chap,' he would reply with a benign smile, but she had the furious feeling that he was only laughing at her. Because once, when she did set out deliberately to madden him by sneering at his conventionality he lost his temper and snapped, 'Superficially is a damn good way to know people.' And this, as she realized, wasn't what he meant either. She suspected that whereas her plumbing of the depths meant that she was continually changing planes in her relations with people, moving rapidly from aloofness to intimacy and back, enthusing and suspecting, he considered only the characteristics that could be handled consistently on one plane. And though it was by its nature inaccurate, she had to admit that it worked, because in the plumbing business you never really knew where you were with anyone.

They had other causes of disagreement, though at first these were comic rather than alarming. Religion was one; it was something of an obsession with Shiela, but on the only occasion when she got him to Mass he sighed as he did when she took him to the pictures and said mournfully as they left the church, 'Those fellows haven't changed in thirty years.' He seemed to think that religion should be subject to the general improvement in conditions of living. When she pressed him about what he thought improvements would be it turned out that he thought churches should be used for lectures and concerts. She did not lose hope of converting him, even on his death-bed, though she realized that it would have to be effected entirely by the power of prayer since precept and example were equally lost on him.

Besides this, there was the subject of his health. In spite of his girth and weight she felt sure he wasn't strong. It seemed to her that the climb from the city each evening was becoming too much for him. He puffed too much, and in the mornings he had an uproarious cough which he turned into a performance. She nagged him to give up the pipe and the whiskey or to see a doctor but he would do neither. She surprised him by bringing the doctor to him during one of his bronchial attacks, and the doctor backed her up by advising him to give up smoking and drinking and to take things easily. Jim laughed as if this were a good joke, and went on behaving in precisely the same way. 'Moderation is the secret,' he said as he measured his whiskey against the light. 'The steady hand.' She was beginning to realize that he was a man of singular obstinacy, and to doubt whether if he went on in this way, she would have him even for the eight years that the Gaffney expectation of life promised him.

Besides, he was untidy and casual about money, and this was one of the things about which Shiela was meticulous.

'It's not that I want anything for myself,' she explained with a conscious virtue. 'It's just that I'd like to know where I stand if anything happens to you. I'll guarantee Paddy won't be long finding out.'

'Oh, begor, you mightn't be far wrong,' he said with a great guffaw.

Yet he did nothing about it. Beyond the fact that he hated to be in debt he did not seem to care what happened to his money, and it lay there in the bank, doing no good to anyone. He had not made a will, and when she tried to get him to do so, he only passed it off with a joke.

Still refusing to be beaten, she invited his solicitor to supper, but whatever understanding the two men had reached, they suddenly started to giggle hysterically when she broached the matter, and everything she said after that only threw them into fresh roars of laughter. Jim actually had tears in his eyes, and he was not a man who laughed inordinately on other occasions.

It was the same about insurance. Once more, it was not so much that she wanted provision for herself, but to a girl who always carried an identification card in her handbag in case of accidents, it seemed the height of imprudence to have no insurance at all, even to pay for the funeral. Besides – and this was a matter that worried her somewhat – the Gaffney grave was full, and it was necessary to buy a new plot for herself and Jim. He made no protest at the identification card she had slipped in his wallet instructing the finder of the body to communicate at once with herself, though she knew he produced this regularly in the shop for the entertainment of his friends, but he would have nothing to say to insurance. He was opposed to it because money was continuously decreasing in value and insurance was merely paying good money for bad. He told her of a tombstone he had seen in a West Cork cemetery with an inscription that ran: 'Here Lie the Remains of Elizabeth Martin who.' 'Poor Elizabeth Martin Who!' he guffawed. 'To make sure she had the right sort of tombstone she had it made herself and the whoors who came after her couldn't make head or tail of the inscription. See what insurance does for you ... Anyway, you little bitch,' he growled good-naturedly, 'what the hell do you always want to be burying me for? Suppose I bury you for a change?'

'At any rate, if you do, you'll find my affairs in order,' Shiela replied proudly.

3

She had sent postcards to Matt from France, hoping he might make things up, but when they returned to Cork she found that he had taken a job in the Midlands, and, later, it was reported that he was walking out with a shopkeeper's daughter who had a substantial fortune. A year later she heard of his engagement and wrote to congratulate him. He replied promptly and without rancour to say that the report was premature and that he was returning to a new job in Cork. Things had apparently not gone too well between himself and the shopkeeper's daughter.

Shiela was overjoyed when at last he called on them in Fair Hill, the same old Matt, slow and staid, modest and intelligent and full of quiet irony. Obviously he was glad to be back in Cork, bad as it was. The Midlands were too tame even for him.

Then Shiela had her great idea. Kitty O'Malley was the old friend of Jim's whose chequered career Shiela had tried to analyse. She was a gentle girl with an extraordinary ability for getting herself entangled with unsuitable men. There had already been a married man who had not liked to let her know he was married for fear of hurting her feelings, a mental patient and a pathological liar who had got himself engaged to two other girls because he just could not stop inventing personalities for himself. As a result, Kitty had a slightly bewildered air because she felt (as Shiela did) that there must be something in her which attracted such people though she couldn't imagine what it was.

Shiela saw it all quite clearly, problem and solution, on the very first evening Matt called.

'Do you know that I have the perfect wife for you?' she said.

'Is that so?' asked Matt with amusement. 'Who's she?'

'A girl called O'Malley, a friend of Jim's. She's a grand girl, isn't she, Jim?'

'Grand girl,' agreed Jim.

'But can she support me in the style I'm accustomed to?' asked Matt who persisted in his pretence of being mercenary.

'Not like your shopkeeper's daughter, I'm afraid.'

'And you think she'd have me?'

'Oh, certain, if only you'll let me handle her. If she's left to herself she'll choose an alcoholic or something. She's shy, and shy girls never get to be courted by anything less dynamic than a mental case. She'll never go out of her way to catch you, so you'd better leave all that to me.'

Shiela had great fun, organizing meetings of her two sedate friends, but to her great surprise Jim rapidly grew bored and angry with the whole thing. After they had been three times to Fair Hill and he had been twice to supper with them, he struck. This time Shiela had arranged that they were all to go to the pictures together, and Jim lost his temper with her. Like all good-natured men, when he was angry he became immoderate and unjust.

'Go with them yourself!' he shouted. 'What the hell do you

want mixing yourself up in it at all for? If they can't do their own courting let them live single.'

She was downcast and went to the bedroom to weep. Soon after he tiptoed into the room and took her hand talking about everything except the subject on her mind. After ten minutes he rose and peered out of the low window at the view of the city he had loved from boyhood. 'What the hell do they want building houses here for and then not giving you a decent view?' he asked in chagrin. All the same, she knew he knew she was jealous. It was all very well arranging a match between Matt and Kitty, but she hated the thought of their going out together and talking of her the way she talked of them. If only Jim had been her own age she would not have cared much what they said of her, but he was by comparison an old man and might die any day, leaving her alone and without her spare wheel. She could even anticipate how it would happen. She was very good at anticipating things, and she had noticed how in the middle of the night Jim's face smoothed out into that of a handsome boy, and she knew that this was the face he would wear when he was dead. He would lie like that in this very room, with a rosary bead he could no longer resent between his transparent fingers, and Matt in that gentle, firm way of his would take charge of everything for her. He would take her in his arms to comfort her and each would know it had come too late. So though she did wish him to have Kitty if he could not have her, she did not want them to be too much together in her absence and hoped they might not be too precipitate. Anything might happen to Jim; they were both young – only thirty or so – and it would not hurt them to wait.

When they did marry six months later, neither Matt nor Kitty knew the generosity that had inspired her or the pain it had caused her. She suspected that Jim knew, though he said no more about it than he did about all the other things that touched him closely.

Yet he made it worse for her by his terrible inability to tidy up his affairs. All that winter he was ill, and dragged himself to the shop and back, and for three weeks he lay in bed, choking – as usual with a pipe that gave him horrible spasms of coughing. It was not only that he had a weak chest; he had a weak heart as well, and one day the bronchitis would put too much of a strain on the overstrained heart. But instead of looking after himself or making a will or insuring himself, or doing any of the things one would expect a sickly old man with a young wife to do, he spent his time in bed, wrapped in woollies and shawls, poring over house-plans. He had occupied his father's unmanageable house on Fair Hill for twenty years without ever wishing to change it, but now he seemed to have got a new lease of life. He wanted to get rid of the basement and have one of the back rooms turned into a modern kitchen with the dining-room opening off it.

Shiela was alarmed at the thought of such an outlay on a house she had no intention of occupying after his death. It was inconvenient enough to live in with him but impossibly lonely for a woman living alone, and she knew that no other man, unless he had Jim's awkward tastes, would even consider living there. Besides, she could not imagine herself living on in any house that reminded her of her loss. That too she could anticipate; his favourite view, his chair, his pipe-rack, emptied of his presence, and knew she could never bear it.

'But you said yourself it was hell working in that kitchen,' he protested. 'And it's awful to have to eat there. It gives you the creeps if you have to go down there after dark.'

'But the money, Jim, the money!' she protested irritably.

'We have the money, girl,' he said. 'That's what you keep on saying yourself. It's lying there in the bank, doing no good to anybody.'

'We might be glad of it one of these days,' said Shiela. 'And if we had to sell the house, we'd never get back what we spent. It's too inconvenient.'

'Who the hell said I wanted it back?' he snorted. 'I want a place I can have some comfort in. Anyway, why would we sell it?'

This was something she did not like to say, though he knew what was on her mind, for after a moment he gave a wicked little grin and raised a warning forefinger at her.

'We'll make the one job of it,' he whispered. 'We'll build the kitchen and buy the grave at the same time.'

'It's no joking matter, Jim.'

He only threw back his head and roared in his childish way.

'And we'll buy the bloody tombstone and have it inscribed. "Sacred to the Memory of James Gaffney, beloved husband of Shiela Gaffney Who." I declare to my God, we'll have people writing books on the Whos. The first family in Cork to take out insurance.'

She tried to get him to compromise on an upstairs kitchen of an inexpensive kind, a shed with a gas oven in it, but he wouldn't even listen to her advice.

'Now, mind what I'm telling you, girl,' he said, lecturing her as he had done on the first night of their marriage, 'there's some maggot of meanness in all Irish people. They could halve their work and double their pleasure but they'd sooner have it in the bank. Christ, they'd put themselves in a safe-deposit if only they'd keep. Every winter of their lives shivering with the cold; running out to the haggard the wickedest night God sent; dying in hundreds and leaving the food for the flies in summer – all sooner than put the money into the one business that ever gives you a certain return: living! Look at that bloody city down there, full of perishing old misers!'

'But Jim,' she cried in dismay, 'you're not thinking of putting in heating?'

'And why the hell wouldn't I put in heating? Who keeps on complaining about the cold?'

'And a fridge?'

'Why not, I say? You're the one that likes ice-cream.'

'Ah, Jim, don't go on like that. You know we haven't enough money to pay for the kitchen as it is.'

'Then we'll get it. You just decide what you want, and I'll see about the money.'

By the following summer Jim, who was behaving as though he would never die, was planning to get rid of the old improvised bathroom downstairs and install a new one of the most expensive kind off their bedroom.

'Jim,' she said desperately, 'I tell you we cannot afford it.'

'Then we'll borrow it,' he replied placidly. 'We can't afford to get pneumonia in that damned old outhouse either. Look at the walls! They're dripping wet. Anyway, now we have security to borrow on.'

But she hated the very thought of getting into debt. It wasn't that she didn't appreciate the fine new kitchen with a corner window that looked over the hill and up the valley of the river, or was not glad of the refrigerator and the heating, and it was certainly not that she wished Jim to die, because she worried herself into a frenzy trying to make sure he looked after himself and took the pills that were supposed to relieve the strain on his heart. No, if only someone could have assured her once for all that Jim would live to be eighty she could have resigned herself to getting in debt for the sake of the new bathroom. But it was the nagging feeling that he had such a short time to live and would die leaving everything in a mess of debt and extravagance as it was now that robbed her of any pleasure she might feel.

She could not help contrasting themselves and the Sheridans. Matt had everything in order. It was true that he did not carry any regular identification card, but this, as she knew was due more to modesty than irresponsibility. Matt would have felt self-conscious about instructing a totally unknown person as to what to do with his body. But he did have as much insurance as he could afford and his will was made. Nothing serious was left unprovided for. Shiela could not help feeling that Kitty owed her a lot, and Kitty was inclined to feel the same. For a girl with such a spotty career it was a joy to be married to someone as normal as Matt.

Not that Shiela found so much to complain of in Jim, apart from the one monstrous fact that he was too set in his ways. She saw that no matter how dearly you loved a man of that age or how good and clever he might be, it was still a mistake because there was nothing you could do with him, nothing you could even modify. She did not notice that Jim's friends thought he was different, or if she did she never ascribed it to her own influence. A girl who could not get him to do a simple thing like giving up smoking could not realize that she might have changed him in matters of more importance to himself. For we do not change people through the things in them that we would wish to change, but through the things that they themselves wish to change. What she had given Jim, though she did not recognize it, was precisely the thing whose consequences she deplored, the desire to live and be happy.

Then came the tragedy of Kitty's death after the birth of her second child. Matt and the children came to stay with them in Fair Hill until Matt's mother could close up her own home and come to keep house for him. Jim was deeply shocked by the whole business. He had always been exceedingly fond of Kitty, and he went so far as to advise Matt not to make any permanent arrangement with his mother but to marry again as soon as he could. But Matt, as he told Shiela on the side, had no intention of marrying again, and though he did not say as much, she knew that he would never remarry at least until she was free herself. And at once she was seized with impatience because everything in life seemed to happen out of sequence as if a mad projectionist had charge of the film, and young and necessary people like Kitty died while old men like Jim with weak hearts and ailing chests dragged on, drinking and smoking, wheezing and coughing and defying God and their doctors by planning new homes for themselves.

Sometimes she was even horrified at the thoughts that came into her mind. There were days when she hated Jim and snapped and mocked at him until she realized that her behaviour was becoming monstrous. Then she went to some church and kneeling in a dark corner covered her face with her hands and prayed. Even if Jim believed in nothing, she did, and she prayed that she might be enlightened about the causes of her anger and discontent. For, however she tried, she could find in herself no real hostility to Jim. She felt that if she were called upon to do it, she could suffer anything on his behalf. Yet at the same time she was tormented by the spectacle of Matt, patient and uncomplaining, the way he looked and the way he spoke and his terrible need of her, and had hysterical fits of impatience with Jim, older and rougher but still smiling affectionately at her as if he really understood the torments she was enduring. Perhaps he had some suspicion of them. Once when he came into the bedroom and saw her weeping on the bed, he grabbed her hand and hissed furiously, 'Why can't you try to live more in the present?'

It astonished her so much that she ceased weeping and even tried to get him to explain himself. But on matters that concerned himself and her Jim was rarely lucid or even coherent, and she was left to think the matter out for herself. It was an idea she could not grasp. It was the present she was living in and it was the present she hated. It was he who lived in the future, a future he would never enjoy. He tried to curb himself because he now realized how upset she became at his plans, but they proved too much for him, and because he thought the front room was too dark and depressing with its one tall window, he had a big picture window put in so that they could enjoy the wonderful view of the city, and a little terrace built outside where they could sit and have their coffee on fine summer evenings. She watched it all listlessly because she knew it was only for a year or two, and meanwhile Matt was eating his heart out in a little house by the river in Tivoli, waiting for Jim to die so that he could realize his life's dream.

Then to her astonishment, she fell ill and began to suspect that it might be serious. It even became clear to her that she might not be going to live. She was not really afraid of something for which she had prepared herself for years by trying to live in the presence of God, but she was both bewildered and terrified at the way in which it threatened to make a mockery of her life and Matt's. It was the mad projectionist again, and again he seemed to have got the reels mixed up till the story became meaningless. Who was this white-faced, brave, little woman who cracked jokes with the doctors when they tried to encourage her about the future? Surely, she had no part in the scenario.

She went to hospital in the College Road, and each day Jim came and sat with her, talking about trifles till the nuns drove him away. He had shut up the house on Fair Hill and taken a room near the hospital so as to be close to her. She had never seen a human being so anxious and unhappy, and it diverted her in her own pain to make fun of him. She even flirted with him as she had not done since the days of their courtship, affecting to believe that she had trapped him into accepting her. But when Matt came to see her the very sight of him filled her with nausea. How on earth could she ever have thought of marrying that gentle, devoted, intelligent man! All she now wanted health for was to return to Fair Hill and all the little improvements that Jim had effected for their happiness. She could be so contented, sitting on the terrace or behind the picture window looking down at the city with its spires and towers and bridges that sent up to them such a strange, dissociated medley of sound. But as the days went by she realized with her clear, penetrating intelligence that this was a happiness she had rejected and which now she would never be permitted to know. All that her experience could teach her was its value.

'Jim,' she said the day before she died, as she laid her hand in his, 'I'd like you to know that there never was anybody, only you.'

'Why?' he asked, trying to keep the anguish out of his face. 'Did you think I believed it?'

'I gave you cause enough,' she said regretfully. 'I could never make up my mind, only once, and then I couldn't stick by it. I want you to promise me if I don't come back that you'll marry again. You're the sort who can't be happy without someone to plan for.'

'Won't you ever give up living in the future?' he asked with a reproachful smile and then raised her hand and kissed it.

It was their last conversation. He did not marry again, even for her sake, though in public at least he did not give the impression of a man broken down by grief. On the contrary, he remained cheerful and thriving for the rest of his days. Matt, who was made of different stuff, did not easily forgive him his callousness.

Frank O'Connor

'A Master' – THE LISTENER

'Perfect' – THE SPECTATOR

Also in PAN is the entrancing story of O'Connor's life as schoolboy, revolutionary and director of the Abbey Theatre.

Sean O'Casey

Sean O'Casey wrote his evocative and richly
entertaining autobiography in six volumes
over more than two decades. Each volume is
essential reading for a proper appreciation of
this major Irish dramatist.

Walter Macken

These and other PAN Books are obtainable
from all booksellers and newsagents. If you
have any difficulty please send purchase price
plus 7p postage to PO Box 11, Falmouth,
Cornwall.
While every effort is made to keep prices low
it is sometimes necessary to increase prices at
short notice. PAN Books reserve the right to
show new retail prices on covers which may
differ from those advertised in the text or
elsewhere.